Murder at Hassle High

Constance Meccarello-Gerson

To my parents who are no longer
with us:
Constantino and Angelina
Meccarello,
        miss you every day.

Acknowledgements
To My UFT writers workshop a
special thanks to Terry Riccardi
my editor, James Cunningham my
teacher, and all the members of
the workshop who listened to it
all.

A special thanks to my Husband,
Alain who read every word.

You can contact the author on her
website
constancemeccarello.com

1
"Is this a Dagger I See Before Me?" (Macbeth)

We all hated her. The whole faculty hated her. Even the students hated her. As a Principal she was not a reassuring type of person, not even nice. To put it more bluntly, she was unjust. She was always complaining about anything the faculty and staff did. She held surprise inspections, and observations. She wrote people up for the slightest rule infraction. Perhaps that is why at 7 a.m. on Monday, June 1, 2016, when I walked into her office for a scheduled meeting to discuss my teaching skills, I was not as shocked as I would have thought, to find her dead. Her office, which was the size of my whole apartment, was a mess. The light in the outer office where her secretary, Sheila, sat was very dim. But the light was on in her inner office; I could see it under her door. I knocked.

"Mrs. Booth?". I called.

There was no reply.

"Mrs. Booth?" I called out louder.

Nothing.

Perhaps she was brewing her evil brew, one of her endless pots of coffee. The woman was addicted to coffee. She drank it all day long. She walked the halls with a cup of black sludge in her hand. I tried the door handle. It opened.

I stepped inside. And ruined my day.

In the middle of her office was a large wooden highly polished conference table. It could easily accommodate twenty people. Booth was seated in a chair at the head of the table, slumped over. Black roots were showing at the top of her dyed blonde head. Funny what you think about when you find a body.

I walked over and touched her. She was very cold. Considering that she typically kept her office at 85 degrees, that told me something. And if that did not do it, the letter opener sticking out of her back did.

I screamed.

No one came. I guessed that the rest of the staff was not in yet. Mrs. Booth's office walls were thick, almost soundproof. I grabbed the desk phone and called 911.

When a calm person answered, I yelled into the phone, "The Principal is dead!"

The female operator said the police would send someone right away, but could I tell them what school I was in?

"Hassle High School, it is on the corner of Kissena Blvd and Union Turnpike in Queens," I said, "and hurry. I'm here alone I think."

The operator said the police would hurry. She then told me to go into a room with a locked door and wait for the police, in case the criminal was still in the building.

I went to the secretary's office and locked the outer door then sat down on the wooden bench. No one could enter unless I unlocked the door or someone had a key. I waited and waited. My mind wheeled around and around. Who could have done this? I sat, waited and listened. And waited some more....

Finally, after at least ten minutes went by, I heard sirens in the distance. They were coming closer and closer and they finally stopped in front of the school, on busy Kissena Blvd.

Footsteps tramped down the hallway at a fast pace. I sat and hoped it was not another teacher who had an appointment after me with Booth. But when I unlocked the door I found a tall dark, handsome Italian looking detective in his early fifties. Really, my perfect fantasy man, if I wasn't already happily married. But I was, happily married, I mean.

I stared at him. He stared at me. We stared at each other. Did he seem familiar?

He spoke. And I knew.

"Hi, I am Detective Joe Viola, "he said. Doesn't it figure he still has those perfect teeth. He flashed his gold shield in my face. "Did you call 911?

"Yes."

He waited looking at me. Suddenly his smile widened. "Maria?"

I nodded. "How you been Joe? It's been a long time."

We both smiled at each other.

"Over 30 years, six months and an odd number of days. But who is counting? Did you find a body?"

"Yes," I ignored the year, month, day, count. Why was he still counting? This from the man who had broken off our engagement a week before the wedding. I quit the police department because I could not stand the thought of working with him every day without an explanation as to why he did not want to marry me. He never gave me one. So, I changed direction got my Master's Degree, then went into teaching. I met Al and we had a real wedding a year later. Life does go on. I still had not answered Joe's question regarding Booth's location. Frankly, I could not believe he was standing in front of me after all these years!

"Where is the body?" Now at this point his smile was fading slightly and his perfect teeth were beginning to look clinched.

I had had it; I mean why was he just standing there? I pointed to Booth's cracked open door.

He took a walk into Booth's office.

I fainted.

When I came to, I was stretched out on the hard, wooden bench with an EMC woman standing over me, a blood pressure machine attached to my arm.

"Is it high?" I was on meds for high blood pressure.

She glanced kindly at me. "No, it's fine. I'm going to tell Detective Viola that you are awake again. I know he has some questions."

Viola, I said to myself, doesn't it figure. I avoided him and the police station all these years after being dumped. It was a little too much. Detective Perfect came out of the inner office. He smiled that perfect smile again in my direction. "Are you OK?" he asked, concern in his voice.

"Yes". I am a child of the 60's and was taught at an early age, to limit my answers to the police, even though I had been a cop, myself. After what Viola had done to me, I planned not to share too much with him.

This time we did not play a waiting game. "Maria, what is your married name?"

I paused, "Maria Bruno-Cohen. I go by Bruno at work." He wrote it down in his notebook.

"Why were you here so early?" He sat down in Sheila's black, Department of Education issued chair and wheeled it over to where I was finally sitting up.

"I had a meeting with Mrs. Booth."

"Why? "

"She observed me teaching in my classroom last week, and she wanted to discuss her observations with me."

"So'" he smiled, "that wasn't a good enough reason to kill her, was it?"

"No" I replied. "I have tenure, and there is always the grievance process, which if you get a bad write up or observation, your Union will help you protest. For some Principals it's better than murder. They hate it so much."

Detective Perfect laughed.

It was a one union member to another union member kind of laugh.

I did not join in.

"Can I go get ready for my classes?"

Viola frowned. "Frankly, you look a fright. I would think about going home. I just called the Superintendent from Booth's office, and he said that you have only one classroom, is that correct?"

I nodded.

"I told him you had fainted and I would be sending you home. He called a substitute teacher, who is on his way, into the school to cover your classes."

"Why do you want to know how many classrooms I have?

"Because, I have to search them. Your classes will be held in the gym once the substitute teacher arrives. I think you should go home for the day. You look like you've had a shock. I will get to you later today with more questions." He glanced at his watch as if I were holding up his ability to proceed with his crime detection skills.

Flash bulbs went off in the Booth's office, blinding me for a second. I blinked. I decided that at this point in our relationship, it was better to agree with him, than to argue. I would consider this our first date in thirty years and behave myself. I would have plenty of time to question the staff, faculty and students in the building to try to find out who killed Mrs. Booth. I didn't include her friends on this list. The woman worked 15 to 20 hours a day, and as far as the staff and faculty knew, she had no friends.

I nodded when Viola asked if I wanted someone to drive me home. I would be good. He yelled for Officer Smith. A good-looking blonde Amazon came to the door. She must have been at least 6 feet tall. She smiled a wolf's smile at me. Viola was smiling at me at the same time. What? Have the police in Queens gone to Charm the Villain School together? "Smith, take Mrs. Bruno home. I don't want her driving herself in case she faints, again."

"Come on," said Officer Smith, "my car is out back."

Oh, parked in the principal's parking space and the principal not even cold. You could have really gotten in trouble for that if she was still alive. Then I rethought, yep, she was cold.

I climbed into the front seat of the unmarked black police car, next to Officer Smith.

"I live at…"

"Yeah, I know."

That was the end of all conversation till we got to the entrance of my apartment building near the courthouse in Queens. She then pushed a Valkyrie blonde curl away from her face and said, "Don't go traveling today OK? Detective Viola and I expect to find you home later. Get a nap. You look a wreck." What a nice girl. Once again, she was smiling.

I climbed out of the car. The 70-year-old doorman, Willie, looked shocked to see me climbing out of a police car at 8:30 a.m. no less. I said "Hi" but kept walking to the elevator. I pushed the button for my floor, got out, and I walked down the corridor past the horrible green walls that the co-op board had decided were so attractive. I let myself into my, I should say, our home, a two-bedroom two bath co-op.

My attractive non-Italian husband, Al Cohen all six foot of him, was in his boxer shorts reading the morning paper with his reading glasses on, in his armchair. His curly grey hair was wet. He must have just come from the shower after going to the gym, where he was trying to get off thirty pounds. Al had retired from teaching this year at age 65. He knew my morning routine cold and was surprised to see me walk in when I should have been in a classroom.

He took one look at my face. "What happened?" His forehead above his reading glasses wrinkled with concern.

"I found Mrs. Booth dead in her office. Viola is the lead detective." Al knew all about Viola. I had told him everything. He frowned. I threw myself on the brown leather couch with my feet up, shoes off.

"How was she killed?"

"She had a letter opener stuck in her back. It was awful." I sighed. He took my head off the end of the couch and held on to it as he sat down with my head in his lap patting it. He really did love me. "I called the police. They sent me home and told me not to go anywhere. Booth was cold when I found her. Do you think they think I did it?"

He smiled. Not the Villain Charm School smile, thank god. "Mary Poppins kills the principal? I doubt it..."

"You think I need a lawyer?"

He frowned. "Not yet. We will see...."

I yawned. "Boy, am I sleepy. But I can't help wondering who got up the guts to do her in."

"Nice," he answered. "Please don't share that thought with the police.... In fact, don't share much with the police. Ok?" He placed my head on a pillow and stood up.

I yawned again. "Ok," I said and fell asleep.

Then I had a dream. In this dream I met the faculty as if for the first time. Could one of them have really committed murder?

2

"My troublous dreams this night doth make me sad" (King Lear)

All of Hassle High's faculty and staff came into focus in my dream. I found myself thinking about each of them and their relationships to each other. I wrote down a few notes the next day about the impressions from that dream.

The Faculty

Mrs. Booth was the principal, back when I joined the faculty 20 years ago. She was in her 50s then. When I went into her office and saw a letter opener sticking out of her back, she was in her early 70s. She had dyed blonde hair, was five-foot one in height, and weighted 90 pounds. Hated by students, faculty and staff equally. When she walked the hall, she commented on a teacher's bulletin boards and how she didn't like them in front of everyone. She never said hello to a student. She would just walk by them as if they did not exist. Custodians and staff were told that the building needed cleaning all the time, even when the floors had just been waxed. If a faculty member did something extra, like chaperone a dance or take students on a trip, Mrs. Booth would always find something that that teacher did wrong.

On the other hand, the English faculty loved Bob Silver the English assistant principal. He was forty years old, 20 years ago. He continuously complemented his teachers on everything they did. The exact opposite of Mrs. Booth. Mrs. Booth, who had inherited him from the former principal, hated him. No one knew why she hated him, but she constantly yelled at him in meetings, and undermined him whenever she had an opportunity. Since he had assistant principal tenure, she could not get rid of him easily.

Marge Largen was a cute English teacher, who started a few days ahead of me. Not a brainy type, she was very much loved by students, something that may have had to in part, with the fact that she was a really easy grader.

Cindy Teller was an English teacher who had hated Booth from the start. Booth walked into her room that first week, did not like Teller's teaching method and argued with her in front of her class. Teller had a principal's license and her father was a superintendent. Rumor had it that Booth owed him a few favors. And so, he made Booth give Teller a job. Booth hated being pressured by the district office.

Candy Thomas was the girls dance and gym instructor and was very fit. Some men on the faculty found her beautiful. The rumor was that she sometimes went out with male faculty in secret. But no faculty member had ever mentioned seeing her with anyone in public. She was mean and had a nasty mouth when crossed. I'd had a few run-ins with her over the years.

Bill Mecca was the Italian teacher born in Naples, Italy. He was dark and good-looking in a sly way, he was a high school girl magnet, very vain and conceited.

Megan Murphy was the Math assistant principal. She was another assistant principal like Bob Silver, with tenure and the lowest math tests scores in the district. She was the cousin of the Mayor of the City of N.Y. and therefore impossible to fire, through Booth had tried many times over the past 20 years. Why she did not transfer somewhere else is beyond belief. Booth was constantly checking her work and the work of her staff. The pressure that Megan was under all the time never ended.

Dickie Somers was the Assistant Principal of security and one of Booth's favorites. He was 24 years old and very cute, but a real piece of work. He spent every waking moment trying not to do his job. Dickie was very lazy and thought he was God's gift to the female staff. If you had a real emergency in your classroom, you would not be able to find Dickie.

The Secretaries and the Custodians

Sheila Moore was the principal's secretary. She knew where all the bodies are buried but, was very close-lipped. She never shared any information about Booth.

Nan Summers was Dickie's secretary, a beautiful bombshell. Many of the faculty thought she might be more than a secretary to Dickie. She was certainly very smart. Nan really ran the office for Dickie.

Rich and Nat were the custodians. They see all, and sometimes share all, with the faculty.

Mrs. Booth introduced me to everyone at the first faculty meeting the first day. It was the only day she was ever really nice to me. Honestly, I did not see her that much, and she probably only came into my room once a year. But, that was enough.

The doorbell rang and I woke up from my nap. Al answered the door. There stood Detective Perfect and his sidekick Officer Smith. Al frowned deeply at Viola. These two would not be friends. I squinted at Viola and Smith from my nest on the couch. I mean could these two people look any more beautiful? They were like a modeling ad for a perfect pair of police officers. Al invited them in. He went from a frown at Viola to a wide smile when he saw Smith. He glanced at me. I could tell he was impressed by her looks. Like I wouldn't notice. I know I had gained a few pounds over the years, Ok more than a few, more like forty, but I still didn't like it too much when Al noticed a beautiful woman like Smith.

Perfect spoke first.

"Ms. Bruno-Cohen. I hope we are not disturbing you, but there are a few facts that we want to check with you."

"OK." I sat up on the couch, "Come on in Detective Viola, Officer Smith. Would you like some coffee?" (Doesn't everyone ask police officers that question? Original, huh?)

"Please come in and sit down." I waved to the living room chairs.

"No coffee for us," answered Perfect. "But we were wondering if you could take us step by step through your morning starting with when you got up and ending with when you discovered the body. Please."

"Sure. I got up about 6 a.m. I had to be at Mrs. Booth's office by 6:45. I showered, dressed, ate a diet chocolate muffin and coffee. I got dressed in my grey suit. I dressed in a suit since I would be seeing Mrs. Booth. Normally I don't wear suits to work. I drove to school. I unlocked the front door with my key. I have a key to the front door since I direct the school play. I need a key because the play rehearsals run late sometimes. I saw her secretary's office door was not locked. I expected it not to be locked, because Mrs. Booth was waiting for me. I entered the outer office and I saw a light on in Mrs. Booth's office. It appeared that she was expecting me. I walked into her office and found her with a letter opener sticking out of her back. She was dead. I did not touch anything in her office but the phone on her desk to call 911. I called 911. I sat in the secretary's office waiting for you. You arrived, we spoke, I fainted. That's it."

Al sat in his chair all ears. I had not gone into such detail since I got home and he was curious, too.

Perfect and sidekick took notes. I remembered from my rookie days on the police force, that only one person on the police team would take notes. But I was wrong and things had changed since I was a cop. Funny what you think about when explaining finding your first murdered body. I had finished describing my day.

Detective Viola stared at me unblinking. I stared back.

Al coughed. "Is there anything else, Detective? My wife is tired."

Detective Viola stood. All glorious six foot something of him. I wish I was not so very happy to see him again! But I was. What did that mean? "I will call you downtown to sign the statement, but I also would like to come back in the morning and hear about the other faculty members."

I stood too. No use letting the police walk all over me, without commenting back, especially when it came to Viola. "I will be in class in the morning. I get home after four p.m. You are very welcome to come by then."

"Well, I will expect you in my office downtown at four p.m. to sign your statement and to tell me what you can about the staff and faculty." He smiled.

I smiled.

Al did not smile. He disliked Viola on sight. No surprise there. He looked back and forth at the two of us. Then he walked the detectives out of our apartment door.

After the door closed, he did not smile at me. "We may need that lawyer. I think they think you killed her."

3

"Thou knowst tis common; all that lives must die" (Hamlet)

It was a terrible night. We argued for hours about whether I should go into school or not. Al thought since I could retire now, it would be a good time to do so. He believed since there was a murder at the school, I should not get involved and just leave. Al really disliked Viola and was afraid that I would get upset seeing him.

"Maria, I really don't want you spending time with the guy who dumped you at the altar," he said.

It wasn't quite at the altar, but I didn't want to argue.

"Viola can only cause you to remember all the bad times in your life. He is not a good person. Mrs. Booth's murder will only get you more involved with him. I don't like it," he said.

"My students need me. Many of them have failed English more than once. I can't quit before the end of the term. I have to get them through the play and Regents." I won the fight. I really wanted to know if I could get Joe Viola to cough up the real reason he decided not to marry me. I finally saw him after all these years, and I had to know! Al didn't need to know this. It could wreak our marriage.

I stood in my mirror before I left home and stared into it at my blonde, highlighted, blunt cut hair, big hazel eyes, and my short, plump form. I dressed with care, in case I ran into Viola. What was I thinking?

The school was in turmoil. Why had I decided to come back? My room was locked and covered with police tape. Dickie Somers, Security Assistant Principal, was by my door. He was frowning.

"Your classes are covered. I am not to let you into your room." He paused for dramatic effect.

I said nothing.

"You can go to the Faculty lounge. If I need you to cover a class, I know where you are."

I still said nothing. I just walked away. Dickie was becoming as much of a pain as Booth had been. Really, if I didn't know that he loved the principal so much for giving him his job, I would suspect him. But, no such luck! Rumor had it that the real reason he got an assistant principal of security job was because his mother and the principal had been schoolgirl chums together.

It was hard to believe that Booth had any friends at all; she was evil and lived at school. One example of evil popped in my head as I stared at Dickie. Mrs. Booth once told Megan Murphy in front of the whole faculty that she was "the stupidest assistant principal she had ever met." Also "the teachers you have hired in the Math department are the stupidest teachers in the city." The faculty in that meeting couldn't believe she said something that evil to Megan, who was really very sweet. Meanwhile, Mrs.

Booth hired Dickie, "The Do Nothing" security assistant principal.

But my thoughts switched to the faculty lounge. Ah, the perfect place to see if I could gather a group of suspects together to discuss what happened. I realized what I was thinking and stopped dead in a hallway.

Did I really believe that I could solve this case faster than Detective Viola, he of the perfect looks? I was beginning to agree with Al that maybe they would try to pin this murder on me. I had to do something to protect myself.

I opened the industrial gray door into the faculty lounge and I was surprised. For the first period of the day, the lounge was packed. Marge Largen, Candy Thomas, and Megan Murphy were all there. A nice group to start my questions with.

Megan jumped up when she saw me. She offered me her chair with a wave. "Are you OK? We were worried about you and the shock of finding Booth dead." Her kind face was a mask of concern.

"I am. I am Ok." Then I smiled at her as I took her chair. (Never turn down a free chair in the faculty room, rule #1) I always really liked Megan. I hope she didn't have anything to do with Booth being dead was my next thought and I mentally kicked myself.

"So," said Candy Thomas, crossing her legs, legs that always seemed to go on for days, "tell us all the gory details."

I've always believed that Candy was a very unfortunate name for any girl. I mean, how could anyone take you seriously? I also knew that that beautiful perfectly sculptured gymnastic body and that nasty mouth were two more reasons why I had never really liked her.

Of course, I smiled at her too. "I am sorry, but the police have forbidden me from talking about it."

Candy frowned back at me. Maybe she'll get wrinkles if she keeps up frowning, I hoped. I decided to take the direct approach. "By the way, Candy, I saw your car in the parking lot when I pulled in at 6:30 a.m. yesterday. You were here very early, I thought that your first class was at 9 a.m.?" I smiled sweetly.

Candy's eyes narrowed. Wrinkles for sure.

"I ran the track yesterday morning. I refuse to lose my figure." She ran her eyes up and down my small, plump shape, as if to make her point. Little did she know that after 50 plus years of living and 30 years of marriage, I could care less.

"Wow!" My lips frozen in a grin, "Jogging huh? Were you alone?"

Now I had the whole room interested. In fact, people were staring at me with their mouths open. This faculty was noted for not asking direct questions. You might get an answer back you did not like.

Candy laughed. "Totally." She stood. "Sorry I can't be here for the rest of the inquisition, but I have a dance class next." She threw her long thick blonde hair over her shoulder, and with perfect posture walked from the room.

The bell rang. Everyone fled, and I faced an empty faculty room.

For the rest of the day I was on my own. I was not included for classroom bulletin boards, teachers' meetings, or any of the other activities. By 2:30, I realized it was deliberate. No one wanted to talk to me. The word had gotten around that I was asking questions. At 2:35, I went looking for my next victim. Not everyone could avoid me all day. I decided that if I was going to attack people with questions, I had better attack those closest to me first. I went looking for Bob Silver, the English assistant principal.

Bob was in his closet of an office. It contained one desk, two chairs, a Xerox machine, a computer and a very small window that a midget could not get out of. It was a very tight squeeze for two people. I maneuvered into the spare seat. He was writing what looked like a teacher observation. He kept the name covered so I could see who he was writing about. He finally looked up.

"Maria, what a pleasant surprise!" His blue eyes sparkled as he smiled. "What can I help you with today?"

"Well, Bob, I said. "Do you think there was anything strange in Mrs. Booth's behavior the past few days?" What am I asking? I better think of a reason why I am asking it. "I noticed that something was wrong the past few days and wondered if you had noticed anything similar?" Boy, did that sound lame.... "I'm going to the police station this afternoon and wanted to know you had any thoughts I should pass on?" He paused and really stared at me. This will never work, I thought.

He coughed." Now that I know someone else noticed, I feel I can tell you what I observed. Perhaps you can pass it on this afternoon."

I smiled and nodded and kept my mouth shut.

"The last few days, Booth talked to me about two things." He paused. "Perhaps they were the same two things she spoke to you about?"

He waited for a reply from me.

"Perhaps," I said mysteriously.

"For the first time in years, she talked about retiring. And she talked about having a ton of money. She said she had discovered a new source of funding. I always thought that she played with the budget and gave herself and certain faculty like Candy, Dickie and Bill a lot of overtime that really was not fair to the rest of the faculty. Almost like they had a scheme together. I mean, where did all the school funding go, if not to her?"

He coughed and broke out in a sweat. "The other thing she mentioned was that when she retired, other members of the faculty would be going along into retirement with her. Then she laughed, as if it was a big joke. I really don't know who she could have been talking about, because no one in the English department has

23

said that they're retiring this year. Everyone on the faculty is basically our age or younger. They're not ready to retire. Has anyone mentioned leaving to you?"

Again, he awaited a reply from me. But my mind at this moment was spinning with all the new information he had just given me.

"Well, have they Maria?" He looked like a beet. Why was my answer so important to him?

I scrambled to my feet. "No, but she gave me the same information she gave you." I made ready to swiftly flee the closet. I had to leave before I said something stupid. "I will pass this on to Detective Viola." I kept moving to the doorway.

"Thanks." His face lit up with the full-voltage Bob smile. "I appreciate that, I really do."

I got out of his office and left the building. I slid into my car for the drive down to the police station in Forest Hills. I had plenty to think about all the way there.

4

Detective Viola's Office

I parked two blocks away from the police station, which was a minor miracle, as anyone would know who has tried to park in Forest Hills. I walked into the police station and stood in front of the reception desk, which had undergone total re-decoration since I worked here.

Everything was gray. The station and the station reception desk were gray, the walls were gray, and the uniform on the young policewoman behind the desk was gray. In fact, it looked good on her.

The policewoman was on the phone. As she hung up, she asked, "May I help you?"

"Yes, my name is Maria Bruno. I am here to see Detective Viola."

"Ok let me call him. Have a seat."

She pointed to some really ugly green chairs in the waiting area.

I took a seat.

The elderly couple next to me was holding hands. I could only imagine what they were there for, a robbery, a stolen car, a missing grandchild? I really had to control myself. My imagination was running wild.

Detective Viola arrived. "Mrs. Bruno-Cohen, please follow me."

We headed for the gray elevator. He pushed the gray button for the third floor. I remembered the third floor well from my days as a young cop. He walked out of the elevator into an empty gray hallway and opened a gray office door to the left. Inside the office was an open area that had partitions. He led me to one partition near floor to ceiling windows. Everything upstairs was painted gray or green. The furniture was gray or green too. He gestured to the green and a grey chair in front of his desk.

I sat.

"So, what can you, tell me about the faculty?"

Of course, he was not going to discuss dumping me before our wedding.

I went into detail describing my first day at Hassle High School 20 years ago. He took lots of notes. He was too far away from me. I could not see what he was doing.

He stopped. "Well did anything happen to you today that you want to share with me? Let's keep in mind this is a murder, not some faculty party game."

Any thoughts I had of sharing what Bob had told me went out of my head. Faculty party game indeed!

I told him about Candy and the car in the lot, when I came to the building the morning of the murder. I told him what I had asked Candy and what she said she had been doing there so early. I skipped Bob totally. I really wanted time to think about what he had told me. I stopped my story at Candy walking out of the lounge.

"Everyone avoided me the rest of the day."

Viola stared at me. We both smiled. "If that is all, I'll get this typed up for you and you can come back and sign it." He paused. "You know of course that I can use all the inside information you get. If you hear of anything that you think I should know about tell me. Don't play cop! You are not a cop anymore." He looked at me uncomfortably.

"Of course not!" My fingers were crossed behind my back.

Detective Viola walked me to the elevator. "Maria, I was glad to see you at Hassle High. It has been too long since we saw each other." He pushed the first-floor button and the elevator door closed. As the door closed, I shut my gaping mouth. What was he saying really? He was happy to see me? What did that mean? I walked to my car and got in. Confused, I drove slowly home.

Al had cooked this absolutely incredible meatloaf that smelled up the hallway of the building when I got home. I told him about my day. He listened, concern on his face and told me to be careful. That night in bed as he snored, I thought and thought and began to come up with a plan.

I decided that I would interview faculty members individually and see what they said about Booth. I would have to be careful, or Viola or Al would have my head. Viola might think I was not a cop but I had been one once. Once a cop, always a cop. With that as my final thought, I fell asleep.

5

Day 2 After the Murder

The Department of Education wasted no time sending a new principal to the school to run things. The newbie principal was all of 25 years old. When he took the stage and introduced himself, the entire faculty looked at each other. We all tried to keep a straight face. The betting sheet hit the rows of teachers' chairs as to how long the newbie would last. The union executive board was collecting a three-dollar per teacher bet by 9 a.m. the next day.

Tommie Newbie introduced himself to all of us and hoped we could put this incident behind us quickly and "have a *great year!*" Incident? What did he mean? Mrs. Booth was a principal for many years and she had been killed. The people in charge of the Department of Education thought of it as "an incident?" Disgusting! While Tommie was going on and on, I glanced at the person next to me.

I had planned to sit next to Megan Murphy. Since I was always early, I had been able to save her a seat next to me. She was assistant principal of the math department, and if there was anyone Booth hated it was Megan. She had tried to get her fired 15 times in the last 15 years. But Megan has a secret weapon. She was the cousin of the Mayor of the City of New York, so the fact

28

that she had the lowest test scores in the district did not matter at all.

Megan was also a bad teacher. The students in all her classes always complained that they were totally confused. She was a lovely, caring person outside of the classroom. One could not imagine her taking a letter opener to Booth, even if Booth made her life miserable in school. Booth had even called her stupid in front of the faculty at a meeting one day.

"Hi Maria, how are you doing?" Megan asked, looking concerned.

"Fine Megan, but I am still upset over finding Booth." No use not getting to the point quickly.

"Yes, I can understand that. But what a hateful woman she was. She hated me you know, and that was all because of the test scores. If she had hired tutors for the library as I'd asked her to, the test scores would have gone up and she would have been much happier."

I thought for a minute. Maybe Megan had a point. All the students who had Megan walked out of her room with totally confused expressions on their faces every day. Maybe good tutors would have at least given them a fighting chance on the tests. Maybe Megan needed teaching course updates, so her students would do better in her classes. What did I know about math? "Did Booth have funds for tutors?"

"Oh yeah, tons of funds. My cousin made sure of that." She was smiling.

This was Megan's eighth school and one could be sure the mayor didn't want her moved again. I mean, how many more high school principals were there in Queens? And how many of them would be understanding of her scores? Not that Booth had understood. Every time she saw Megan in the hall she yelled at her about something.

Megan looked me directly in the eye. "Maria, who could really stab Booth? I mean, to stab someone to death? It really takes a certain kind of person to do that.... even if you hate someone...."

"I agree. But, if you could pick anyone to do it, who would it be?" I was really curious to hear her reply.

"I think it is somebody who we wouldn't normally think would kill her. It had to be someone with something to gain." She looked at me sadly.

The faculty meeting ended. The newbie left the stage. A subdued faculty filed out to their classrooms.

My room was still locked. Someone was covering my classes. The police were not done searching my room and interviewing my students. Interviewing the "Nut Squad" should be very interesting. They are my 10th graders. The reason they are called the "Nut Squad" is that they have failed 10th grade at least twice, and they are usually out of control in the classroom.

The "Nut Squad" is full of gang members and students with problems.

Anyway, it gave me more free time, and I decided to interview Dickie Somers, Assistant Principal of Security.

That is, if I could find out where he was hiding. He made a habit of hiding with his walkie-talkie, so he doesn't have to do any work. A walkie-talkie could cover a lot of mistakes. He could say on the walkie-talkie he was busy in another part of the school, when there is a fight. But while the fight was going on, Dickie was in his office drinking coffee. Boy, what many teachers in this building would not give for a walkie-talkie. Dickie used to speak to his deans, the office, etc., and could really be anywhere in the school. Now, where would I hide if I were Dickie?

I headed for the basement. In the basement were ten classrooms and a whole group of rooms for the union rep, artist's rooms, and five or six rooms for the custodians.

Why would I think the Assistant Principal of Security was hiding in the custodians' rooms? First of all, no one would look for him there. Booth had a fear of being below ground, something to do with "going to Hell." She never came down to the basement even to observe the teachers who taught there. She also called the basement the dungeon. "Never observe a teacher in the dungeon" was her rule. She would wait to observe you when you had a class upstairs.

For a guy who likes to do as little as possible, it was the perfect place to hide. And the reception on the walkie-talkies was not perfect in the basement. You could always claim you did not hear the frantic calls from upstairs. This truly made it the perfect hideout.

In the corner of the head custodian's office Dickie sat, with his feet up on the desk. He did not move an inch when I walked in. He just smiled his lazy, sexy smile, which I am sure worked on girls his age, but I am not his age, I sat. "When do you think I will be able to get back my students and my room?"

"Gee whiz, Maria, I don't know. The police aren't telling me anything."

"So, Dickie," I was no longer being subtle, "who do you think had it in for Mrs. Booth?"

He was shocked. He pulled his feet off the desk. "Well gee, Maria, I don't know. I can't imagine anyone hating that nice woman so much."

My eyes must have bugged out of my head. But I realized he knew a kinder, gentler Booth than the rest of us did. He was the son of one of her best friends, so the rumor went, if you can imagine Booth having best friends or any friends at all.

"Dickie, please take a guess as to who could have done this. I heard through the grapevine that she said she was retiring, and with a lot more money than she thought she had at first. Does that ring any bells with you?"

'Yeah, well gee, the money thing you just mentioned, she mentioned to me. I really don't know more about it than that. I thought maybe she was adding more money to her pension." He was breaking out in a sweat, too, just like Bob. What was it with my questions that caused that reaction? "But, ah gee, did you hear about the *death* threats?"

Death Threats! I shook my head no, kept my mouth shut and waited.

"Well, she had been getting death threats the last three weeks or so. They were all the same. The letters looked like they were cut out of the New York Times. They all said the same thing and they were mailed to her every day. They always said: WE ARE GOING TO BOMB YOU."

"Did you tell the police?"

"Nope. It's probably a kid, and nothing came of it."

Except that she is dead. Why did he not call the police and let someone know?

"I gave her my parking space when she insisted on it. I gave it to her, and every day after school, she made me start the car for her. She was afraid it would explode. Not that I ever believed it would" He sighed. "She was so scared she made me do that."

I was talking to an idiot. I mean, what man goes out every day and starts a car for a woman who is getting bomb threats and then does not tell the police? And his job is head of security!

I smiled. "Wow, Dickie, you are a brave guy!" What a putz, I thought.

"As far as the faculty goes, I think some people did not really like Booth."

"Like who?"

"Sheila is the one you should talk to, because she knows everything about Booth."

"But Sheila liked Booth, who do you think did *not* like her?"

"Megan hated Booth for giving her an "Unsatisfactory" rating."

I knew that already. I wanted new info from Dickie.

"What else? Come on, you spent hours with the woman." I did not add, "behind locked doors with Do Not Disturb sign up." What had been going on in there?

Now I sounded like Viola. I hoped Dickie was dumb enough not to ask why I wanted to know. He was.

"Maybe you should ask Mecca about his young girls." He smiled at me with a slimy expression. Then he gave me a strange look. "Why are you so interested in this? She didn't love you either."

I gulped. I had thought that at least she liked me. "I found her dead, and that has upset me."

"Yeah," he said his eyes turning to slits as he stared at me. "Who isn't? I'll never have that kind of relationship with the new guy. See ya."

He closed his eyes, leaned back in his chair with his feet up on the desk. His walkie-talkie went off, announcing a riot and a fist fight on the first floor. He didn't move an inch.

But I beat a hasty retreat. I went looking for Bill Mecca.

I found him in his classroom in the language wing of Hassle High, surrounded by what looked like senior girls. They were all chatting in Italian and laughing.

From the doorway I studied Bill. He was tall, dark and handsome in an Italian kind of way, but there was something sneaky about him.

Something scandalous. I always thought from my first year that there was something about his interest in young teenage girls that was not safe. He was surely heading for a problem if you asked me. One of these days when he walked down the hallway with his arm around a 17year old cutie who decided to report his behavior to the principal, who then had an angry parent in her office, because his cutie daughter was touched by a teacher... But, years had gone by, and so far, nothing had happened. Bill must have a guardian angel or a charmed life. It was truly amazing!

The girls glanced at the doorway, saw me waiting, and left the room as a bunch, laughing and giggling. I found myself alone with Bill. He smiled. I didn't know where to start. I really should have thought of something to say before I came into the room. I could have kicked myself.

"Hi Bill." Great opening.

"Hi Maria."

"Bill, I'm very upset over finding Booth dead. How do you think such a thing could have happened to her?"

During our whole careers as teachers, I had never asked two questions of Bill. My appearing at his classroom door must have been a shock to him. We were in the faculty room for off periods (preps) together, but I don't think in all our combined years of teaching we ever had a real conversation. It took a while for his response. He stared at me before answering, probably wondering why I was in his classroom and what I was doing asking him anything. But his decent Italian upbringing took control. He had been taught to answer his elders.

"You know, of course, that she had problems with a couple of teachers? "

"Yes. But, Bill, everyone had problems with her. Can you name a specific faculty member? I know a few she had problems with, but do you know any I don't?" Boy, were we both fishing around the issue or what? What a lame conversation.

Bill's face screwed up and he seemed to be thinking about my question. He seemed to be following my crazy logic.

"I get it, you know what happened to Cindy?"

"Nope," I flopped down in one of his student chairs. This could take a while I thought. My feet were killing me. And Bill always liked to go on and on when he told a story.

Cindy had a major disagreement with Dickie over the fact that she had three students who had a fistfight in her room and when she called security, no one came. She had to step in between the students and stop the fight, which the union does not want teachers doing. Of course, they don't want them getting hurt. And, that's just what happened. One of the students punched her in the eye. She had quite a shiner. She went to Booth, who told her to fill out an accident report. But Cindy really went to Booth to complain about Dickie. In true Dickie fashion he had sat around and done nothing, Booth wasn't buying it. She said that Cindy had not called Dickie. Cindy had called Dickie. But it was Cindy's word against his. How could she prove it?

Dickie, when confronted by a socked Cindy, denied the call. Hot nasty language was exchanged. Booth then called Cindy back in the office and yelled at her for yelling at Dickie. Then Cindy yelled at Booth, because here was Cindy with a black eye. And in Booth fashion, she blamed Cindy for the whole thing, saying that Cindy lacked classroom discipline. That lack of discipline is what Booth said led to the fight.

Cindy lost it. She went to the union rep and reported Booth, Dickie and the students. Then Cindy called her father, her father called Booth, and it became a really big deal. But Cindy's father had retired. And Booth had a lot of political pull downtown.

It looked like the only one who would lose was Cindy. When she found out little or nothing would be done about Dickie, she went back into Booth's office and the argument started again. Bill said he just happened to be in the hallway when he heard Cindy in the office yelling," I could kill you!" and storming out the door.

"Well that's it," Bill said. "I told Detective Viola about it. What do you think?"

My reaction was that Bill either spend his non-teaching time with lovely young female students or listening at doorways. In the future, I would be sure to check behind my closed doors. I was floored. I couldn't image Cindy killing an ant, no less Booth. I remembered back to a time when we had shared a classroom together. Cindy would catch flies and release them out the window. I could see her getting angry, but not killing Booth. "I really can't imagine Cindy doing it."

"Neither can I, but she is a possibility," said Bill.

But I was beginning to wonder about Bill. What kind of person was he? The bell rang and I had to go.

"But, who knows? Come back tomorrow. I will know more."

He will know more about what? In Bill's doorway seventeen-year-old girls on a mission to speak to him suddenly surrounded me. I wandered down the hall past crowds of students in a minor daze, thinking about what Bill had told me. I would have to speak to Cindy. I would have to speak to Bill again. But then the 3 p.m. bell rang and I headed for my car in the faculty parking area.

6

Not So Sweet Candy

Al was out with his aquarium fish group for dinner and a fish auction when I got home. He would not be coming home for hours. I was on my own. I heated a low-calorie dinner and sat down to write a plan up as to how I would interview Candy Thomas the next day. As I put pen to paper the phone rang. The caller ID said it was the local police department. I secretly hoped it was Viola. Years ago, I really enjoyed our long phone calls to each other. It was Officer Smith.

"Hi Mrs. Bruno-Cohen. Detective Viola and I were wondering how you are doing?"

"Fine."

"Good, Detective Viola said to remind you that you should not play cop."

"I won't," I mumbled into the phone.

"Great. Detective Viola said to tell you if you get any information about the murder from the faculty, you are to tell him immediately. Good Night."

"Good Night!"

Good grief! He couldn't call me himself, one Italian to another? What was wrong with him? Maybe Mr. Perfect was not so perfect after all....

39

Back to my list of questions for Candy. Why does she jog so early in the morning, and why at school? Was she too cheap to belong to one of those local ritzy gyms? At a ritzy gym she could have met some eligible young men. Why didn't she belong to one? Would she keep her job now that Booth was gone? What would the newbie principal have to say about that? In the current climate of higher education, gym teachers were the first teachers being let go.

Why was a woman who looks the way Candy looks never married? Too good looking? There were a few really good-looking single men in the building; why are there no rumors about her? Why does she go to all the school functions, faculty picnics, and year-end faculty parties alone? What is wrong with her? Woo…. Getting away from the murder now into matchmaker territory…

Better to think about Booth and Candy. Who named a girl Candy anyway? What was her relationship with Booth? How did they get along? Booth recently got a $100,000 grant for Candy's advanced placement dance classes for supplies, books, computers and visiting dance artists. How did Candy spend that? And was it a grant for more than $100,000? If so, had Booth been lining her pockets with grant money for her retirement fund?

Boy, tomorrow would be interesting. ……
What, was it 1030 already?!

Time to go to bed. Where was Al? Buying all the fish in Queens for his tanks?

The next morning, when I got to school, I was able to get into my classroom. The yellow tape was down. During a prep period, I rushed to the upstairs faculty room, where Candy hung out. Marge Largen was there, but no Candy.

I asked Marge, "Any idea where Candy is?"

"Yeah," she replied, "in her room setting up one of those new computers that Booth got her from the grant. I think Dickie is with her."

"Thanks," I said. Ah, a two-for-one sale. Who could ask for more? I hurried to Candy's room. There is never a moment to waste during a prep in high school.

I got to Candy's door, which was open. But before I walked in, I'm afraid I snooped and listened to what was being said between her and Dickie.

"No, "said Candy, "with this heat from the cops I can't meet you as we planned. You'll just have to wait."

"Wait?" whined Dickie, "I don't want to wait!"

Candy's high heels sounded, clack, clack, and clack, as she headed for the door. "You will have to, and like it! Besides, we have to move things in the morning early. I can't be exhausted for that."

I walked in the door. What things needed to be moved? Gym equipment? I couldn't imagine Dickie moving gym equipment even for sexy Candy. "Oh hi, guys, I was just passing by," I said with a great big smile on my face.

Candy's eyes narrowed.

Dickie looked unhappier than usual.

"How's the computer setup going? Candy, I was thinking of joining you for jogging in the morning. I'm gaining some weight.... Want to be jogging buddies?"

I never even walked fast to my car after dismissal. I hadn't run a step-in years. I was silently praying she would say no.

Dickie's mouth fell open.

I guess my suggestion was not subtle and he did not believe me. I waited.

Candy was squinting at me with her eyes like slits. Here it comes, I thought. Well, I did give her the perfect chance.

"Maria, a little weight is not how I would phrase it."

That came from Ms. "I have never gained a pound since *High School*." Candy actually looked me up and down like you would a horse you were planning to buy.

"I think you would do better starting at lunch walking the track. In fact, I would skip lunch, if I were you and just walk the track..."

What a nice girl. Well, I did have it coming.... What the heck was wrong with Dickie? Why did he look so shocked?

"Yeah, you're right, say, who do you run with in the morning? Maybe when I build up my speed from the college track team, I can join you."

I would not have been water carrier on my college track team.

Dickie still looked like he had eaten one of Al's goldfish.

"College track team? Oh yeah, sure. When you build up some speed, come see me and we will see about joining my group. Now Maria, I hate to cut off this brilliant discussion, but I have to finish with Dickie and I have a class in a few minutes."

She then slammed the door in my face!

So much for collegiality.

Hum. Interesting.... Maybe I *did* have something to follow up on. What were they moving?

As I walked back to my room, I asked myself why the secrets? Who was she going jogging with? Why did Dickie look guilty? Was he her jog buddy? What! That can't be it. And what is with Candy going it alone to every school function? I wonder if all of this leads back to the grant money somehow.

7

The Nut Squad Weighs In

"Hey man!" shouted Roberto as I came into the room. Roberto always called me "man". I have tried to correct him, but in three years of his repeating 10th grade it had been no use.

Mrs. Booth came up with a great idea for Roberto this year, why not give him the lead of Hamlet in *Hamlet* the school play? She seemed for some reason to like Roberto. He seemed to be the only student in the school, who spent his free time with her in her office. No one knows what they were doing in there. Roberto never said. After all, Booth ordered me, Roberto playing Hamlet would improve his English grades. I am the director of that brilliant stage project, and who was I to argue with the boss? What a brilliant idea!

So, I spent a good deal of my time emailing Roberto's parents to make sure he showed up for each rehearsal, and calling and texting Roberto's phone, to make sure he showed up for each rehearsal. Thank goodness the play was almost upon us. (Thinking about opening night was giving me hives.)

"Hi, Roberto."

"Man, we want to know, the Boothie person is dead?"

The whole room stopped talking and throwing paper balls at each other and stared at me, waiting for an answer.

"Yes, the principal is dead."

"Is Mr. Somers taking over?"

"Or," piped up Mary, "is Ms. Thomas taking over? "

"Or," jumped in Jeff, "is Ms. Thomas over Mr. Somers? "

The whole class snickered.

"What?" Had they noticed something?

"Oh man Teach," said Roberto, "the whole school knows that Somers and Thomas are doing the evil deed... Like Ms. Thomas has been seen in the locker room after her morning runs with Somers and Mecca by the senior gym classes. They are really close, and she's also been seen with them both, and these guys don't seem to be running to catch her. If you know what I mean, I mean, they caught her already."

The class exploded.

"All right!" I yelled, "Take out your books!"

It took me ten minutes to get some sort of order. The rest of the period, while they worked on some handouts as a quiz, I thought about my three fellow teachers. I firmly believe that kids notice a lot more about teachers than we give them credit for. But in high school *SEX* is a great topic for discussion. I wondered if what my Nut Squad noticed was real, or just what they wanted to be real? I was getting quite confused and decided to run all this (no pun intended) by Detective Viola.

But first, this afternoon, joy, oh joy, was play rehearsal...

8

"To Die, to Sleep" (Hamlet)

The entire cast of misfits and I were all
assembled in the auditorium for rehearsal by 3:30
that afternoon. We were starting the tech
rehearsal process for opening night, two long
weeks away. The lighting people were in the
auditorium stringing lights. They were honors
students. A few cast members were playing guitar
on stage and Ophelia, had just sang through the
wedding of Hamlet's parents. Martha Turnbunk
had a lovely singing voice. I had added a song
into the wedding scene, to showcase the Nut
Squad's musical talent. The Nut Squad had a few
students who could play guitar beautifully.

I kept thinking we should have done a musical.
But, Mrs. Booth wouldn't let me do a musical.
She wanted classics. So, here we were, we had
just finished the scene where the Ghost appears to
Hamlet. "I am thy father's spirit" etc., and
Roberto as Hamlet had just said his first "Hey
man, I am the spirit too" of the rehearsal. Which
meant he was not sure of his lines in the scene. I
was musing, how Hamlet had 4000 more lines to
go, I mean how long could two more weeks of
torture be anyway?

When suddenly, all the lights in the auditorium
and on stage went dark, and I mean dark, like
totally. The school auditorium had no windows
and was like a huge dark box with 2,000 seats.

Then all my misfits started to scream. Who could blame them? I wanted to yell myself, so I did. "Quiet! Use the lights on your cellphones! Is everyone Ok?"

Faint low lights came on as every misfit pulled out their "forbidden in school for any reason" cellphone and lit them up.

Ophelia, Hamlet's love interest and Roberto's main squeeze in real life, another of Mrs. Booth's brilliant casting ideas, ("they will be so cute together"), came out on stage with her cellphone lit up. Of course, Mrs. Booth had given no thought to me. Little did she know how often I spent during a rehearsal in many a dark corner of backstage stopping these two students from having sex, and to make sure all the students had their clothes on. Martha started to scream and scream and scream. The stage was still dark; I could not see what was making her so upset. I walked swiftly up to the front of the apron, toward the stairs to get up on stage, my cellphone light faintly shining. And then I saw him, Roberto, our Hamlet, with what looked like a stage dagger sticking out of his chest.

"Very funny Roberto, get up."

He did not move. Ophelia was still screaming as I climbed the steps to the apron, one of the side doors to the outside opened and closed. I did not see who left the auditorium; I was focused on Roberto, who did not seem to be moving. I walked over to him and realized there was blood everywhere. I checked to see if he was breathing.

There was no pulse. I walked to stage down left exit, opened the door slightly to get cellphone reception, and for the second time that week, called 911.

I sat down in the doorway in shock, and waited for the police to show up. I watched bunches of exiting teachers across the parking lot leaving the building and going to their cars. They were too far away for me to yell to them for help. I thought about teachers and their students. As much as teachers are sometimes angry with students, I did not know one teacher who would kill one. Who would kill a young man with his life ahead of him? I could not believe Roberto was dead.

The children, came and stood outside with me. They bunched together as kids do when they are shocked. It was too freaky to be in the auditorium now, not with Hamlet really dead onstage. Horato and Ophelia came out together. Jeff Sona played Horatio; he was a close friend of Roberto's and he was holding Martha (Ophelia) up; she was still crying.

In the distance, sirens were screaming and coming closer. I stood up, very confused. I mean, why kill Roberto? What could he know that he didn't share with all his bros and multiple friends? The kid could not keep quiet for two minutes. Roberto could never keep a secret. It was just plain strange, and frightening.

If Roberto were dead, how many of my Nut Squad kids were also in danger? These were not the brightest kids. This could be very dangerous for them, and for me! I would have to talk to these students individually and privately, I told myself as the cop cars came into the parking lot. I really had to get to the bottom of this quickly, before someone else died. I watched as Viola and the newbie principal walked toward us.

9

The Show Must Not Go On

It was a long night. We were all taken to the police station in Forest Hills, and I, a police officer and the newbie principal spent a lot of time calling parents to come pick up their children. The police did not think it was safe to wait at the school while they combed room by room, looking for a killer. I didn't blame them; I didn't want to wait in the school either. I had spent a bit of the day fixing up my room, which had been taken apart in the police search when Booth died, so I was not happy to think I had to do it again. But rather a messy room than another dead student, or dead me! I felt much safer at the police station calling upset parents.

The newbie principal was dripping sweat as each parent picked up their child and spoke to him. He had insisted on meeting the parents himself and explaining the situation. Who was I to try to help him or insist that I should explain things? That's why he made the big bucks! But he did drive with Smith to Roberto's home to tell his parents what had happened to Roberto, which was very nice of him actually. Besides I was exhausted just making phone calls. Especially the one I made to my very upset husband who was on his way here with dinner for me. I was starving, and there were 10 more Shakespearean actors to return home. After dinner, I would have to see Viola, who said "*Must* talk to you before you go anywhere." Joyful! I could not wait.

At last, upset parents had picked up all the students and finally Al walked in with a bagel with cream cheese and a diet coke for me. He looked just like the last upset parent who had left the station. Tommy newbie walked over, and he introduced himself to my not newbie husband. Then he turned to me. "Ms. Bruno, I will not be expecting you in school tomorrow. I am giving you the day off, and I think we should cancel the play."

Gee, there's a thought, since Hamlet is in the city morgue. "Well, thank you," I said, "I think you made the right decision regarding the play. Also thank you for speaking to all the parents."

Tommy newbie stood a little straighter. "I appreciate that," he said, "I will see you the day after tomorrow." He looked at Al. "Nice to meet you," he said.

Al said the same, and Tommy walked off into the sunset and possibly the nearest yuppie bar in Forest Hills.

I started wolfing down my bagel and diet coke, a dieter's dream come true, bread! I was very hungry. Al took a chair next to me, one of those green vinyl cop chairs that were scattered throughout the building. He was not happy. "Maria," he said, "I seriously want you to think about retiring."

I kept eating.

Al just looked at me. He could tell I was not going to discuss this here. I looked at him and smiled. "Honey," I said, "I will think about it." I could no more leave the school now than fly to the moon. One of my students was dead. OK, he wasn't the smartest or the most artistic student I had ever had, but he was mine. And now, he was dead. Someone should pay for that.

Before we could discuss this further. Detective Viola appeared. "May I talk to you both in my office." He turned and led the way. Eek, no friendly Italian vibes in that request. We followed him into the elevator and up to his office. It was a long, quiet ride. We sat in his office.

"Mr. Cohen, I am going to ask Maria to tell me in detail about her day and the rehearsal. I hope that you will not comment while I talk to her," Detective Viola said.

"I am as interested in her day as you are, and I don't plan to comment," answered Al.

Both of them looked at me. I started with breakfast, and I told about what the Nut

Squad had said in class regarding Candy,
Dickie and Bill. The three of us were not
sure about the rumor that Candy and Dickie
were having an affair. That is what the Nut
Squad was telling me. Children sometimes
see things. They then make up a rumor. I
then described the rehearsal, the lights going
out, the side door letting someone out,
Ophelia screaming. Roberto dead. How I had
tried to see if he was still breathing. And how
we all went outside and waited for the police.

When I stopped, Detective Viola asked,
"Did you see anyone strange around the
stage? Were there any adults who did not
belong in the auditorium?"

I answered, "When I direct, I sit close to the
front of the stage so if there is a problem I can
be on stage quickly. Someone could have
come in in back of me and I would not have
noticed. There are side doors that lead
outside. If a faculty member has a key, they
can get in and up into the backstage. Unless
the kids told me, someone was backstage, I
would not know that someone was there.

There are four teachers who were assisting
me. Candy is working on lights and set. Bob
is overseeing the program, he is my chairman.
Rich, a social studies teacher, is in charge of
backstage, and trying to keep kids in line, as
is Tom, another social studies teacher. Megan
is working on costumes. I am not sure who
was there today. This murder took place just

about 15 minutes into my rehearsal. No students spoke to me about a teacher in the back. But they are used to teachers being backstage. Someone may have been backstage and the cast may not have mentioned it to me." I stopped talking and looked at Viola. I had nothing more to say. He was looking at his notes.

He looked up. "Were there any students missing from rehearsal?"

I shook my head no.

"Were there any students missing after you found Roberto and everyone went outside?"

Again, the answer was no.

"Well, that is all for now. If you think of anything else, or anything that is strange, let me know."

We all stood. He rang the elevator button, ushered us in and said "Good night."

Al and I were silent on the way home. I was exhausted; he was upset. When we got home I poured a stiff scotch, headed for the shower, and then went to bed.

10

Retire, Said Al.

Breakfast smells reached my unconscious brain. Bacon and coffee were the strongest. I woke up. I threw on a robe and walked out to the kitchen. Al was at the table, coffee cup in hand and rolled up Times in the other. "Ah," he said, "you are awake." I poured coffee, kissed him, and sat down.

He glanced at me, setting the paper between us. We always shared it. "Maria, I want you to retire. I am afraid of whoever is committing these murders, and I am afraid for your safety."

I sipped coffee. "I understand, but a student of mine is dead. I must at least see it through to the end. I really need to know what is going on."

"Needing to know is one thing, working to find the killer is another."

I know, I'll be careful." I rose to get dressed for work. I did not care that the principal had given me the day off. I did not want a day off. I wanted some answers, and the students or faculty might have them.

Al sighed and opened the unopened paper. He had given up arguing with me for the moment.

I grabbed a diet breakfast muffin and left the house for work.

11

The Interviews

I got to the school parking lot and there was Detective Joe Viola leaning against an unmarked car, as if he was waiting for me just like he had when we had dated years ago. I parked, shoved the last of the muffin in my mouth, swallowed and got out of the car, brushing the crumbs off my clothes. He stood leaning against his car and watching me as I locked up.

"Good Morning Joe," I said.

"Good morning. Maria, you know the workings of the school better than I do. Would you mind sitting in on some interviews with me?"

My heart thumped. How exciting! An attendee at a police grilling! Viola did not have a clue that I would not miss this for the world! "Of course, if you think I could be any help?"

"Great!"

We walked together into the school.

"How about during your third period prep? There is a substitute teacher in your room now, can you have her cover your third and fourth period classes? Meet me in the faculty conference room, the Principal has turned it over to me as an office."

"Great! I am sure having my classes covered will not be a problem." We smiled at each and went our separate ways. Gosh, he is still cute! How could I be thinking that, after the man dumped me?

He looked to be heading to his conference room and I was on my way to my first class. I was going to spend my teaching time pumping the students about Roberto and anything else they knew about the deaths. But first, I wanted to stop by Mecca's classroom to see if he had learned anything.

12

Little Pitchers Have Big Ears

Bill Mecca was actually writing on the board when I stopped by his classroom. In 20 years, I don't think I'd ever walked by his room and seen anything on the board. I was shocked. Was he trying to impress the newbie principal? He waved me in and kept writing.

"The principal is coming by today. I'm putting up my lesson plan."

"Oh dear…" This class should be a shocker for the newbie principal, seeing all the girls mooning over Mecca.

"Yeah," he grinned, "guess I'm the lucky one."

Why is the newbie principal observing teachers after a murder in the school yesterday? He must have a screw lose. Who does that to teachers after a shock? I planned to grill the students in my classes. I hoped he would not come by my room.

"I spoke to a few of my girls and they said that Roberto had a habit of listening to faculty conversations outside the doorways. He told the girls he was in the know, but you can't tell with kids, they may or may not be telling the truth. He may have said it to impress the girls. Or the girls may not be telling me the truth either." He shrugged. "Who knows?"

"Did the girls mention what was said?"

"Yeah, a little, they said that Roberto said Candy and Dickie were really chummy on the track in the mornings, and that they went into the boys' locker room together after their morning jogs. Also, that he had seen the two of them together at the local diner where he worked at night. He was a busboy there and did not wait on tables, so he could not overhear them, but he saw them together. He mentioned that he heard Candy was in trouble with Booth, something about money. That's all my girls said."

I thanked Mecca for the information. I bit my tongue to stop myself from warning him to try to stay away from young teenage girls. I walked down the hall with a lot to think about before my classes started.

I got to my room and sent the happy relieved substitute teacher to the office until third period. I sat down at my desk. If the principal came by, I would tell him I was too nervous to be observed. What could he do? Fire me? I have tenure! I awaited the arrival of the Nut Squad. Thirty out of thirty-four came to class. I was amazed. I stood. "So," I asked, as I shut and locked the door, "Why Roberto?"

Twenty voices spoke at once. "Quiet!" I yelled. "One at a time. Hands please!"

Mary, who played the Queen in *Hamlet* took the lead. She removed the earplugs from her ears. "Well, we figure like Roberto saw or heard something at his gang he shouldn't of, or at school."

Gang? Oh no, not gangs!

Jeff jumped in. "Na! not de gang. It must have been something at school. The gang would have killed him on gang turf."

What a pleasant thought. These youngsters lived in a different world than I had growing up in upstate New York.

Jeff continued. "It had to be something at school. Teach, Roberto had a big mouth."

The students in my class nodded. Jeff had a point.

Martha spoke up; she had tears in her eyes. I wondered if she had stopped crying from last night.

"I think we should find out who he talked to this week."

"I don't think that's a good idea. The police are here in the building looking for Roberto's killer. I don't want any more students hurt. Do nothing!"

The bell rang before I could continue. Jeff winked as he left the class. "Leave it to us, Teach." He picked up his guitar and played softly as he walked out of my room.

This was one bad idea, I thought, as the Nut Squad raced out the door. I said a quick prayer that my class would not get in trouble and that no one would get hurt. I got up and walked down to the faculty lounge, to see who was there. I walked into an empty lounge. No one was there. I really do not ever remember this happening, not even on that day when Booth observed twenty teachers for five minutes each and wrote them all up.

What a day that had been! They were all in here whispering to each other as if Booth had wired the faculty room, which some teachers thought she had. Everyone who had been observed was white faced. It had been a real eye-opener that day for the faculty. They really hated her after that. No one could believe that she could get away with doing this, writing everyone up and having the observations count.

Had that been only a month ago? I thought wearily as I fell into a chair. With Booth's death and the death of Roberto last night, it seemed a year ago. What did I know exactly? Someone hated Booth. I guess the easier list would be, who liked her? Someone hated Roberto. Maybe not, hated, but feared what he knew. The most likely people so far were Cindy who argued with Booth about Dickie, and Candy and Dickie who may be having an affair.

My thoughts came back to Bill. What did the Italian teacher know that perhaps he was not sharing with me? Were his girls reliable? Was he honest, or was he scared, too? Scared that too much information might come out about him and the female students?

What about Cindy and her argument with Dickie and Booth? Why didn't Cindy ever come to me about this? She had many moons ago, been my student teacher. I thought we had always been close, at least until Bill blabbed to me yesterday. But why had no one but him heard about this? Sneaky Bill….

Candy and Dickie what exactly was going on there? What had I overheard yesterday? Was it about an affair or about Booth and money, or about both? I was so confused. Maybe meeting Viola would help me find some information.

13

Day One in the Interview Room

I walked down to the faculty conference room on the first floor. It was huge with a beautiful old wooden conference table in the middle, surrounded by beautiful wooden chairs. At the head of the table sat Detective Viola. To his right sat Officer Smith, notebook open. Smith patted the chair next to her and I sat. In came Cindy. I smiled. She smiled. Officer Smith waved her to the other end of the table. She sat down. Viola started with his questions.

"How well did you know Principal Booth?" Cindy sat back in the chair. She did not look nervous to me. "My dad knew her better than I did. I found her difficult and sometimes impossible to work for, but I think everyone did."

"Why?

"She yelled at people. She never had a positive thing to say to anyone, except Dickie. She tried to make you feel small as a teacher and as a person. She was a control freak. I guess that covers it."

Wow! Cindy had a way with words. She hit the nail on the head describing Booth's personality.

"Someone overheard you say that you would kill her. Did you?"

"Ha! Someone who? A faculty member who listens at doors? You should talk to Bill or Dickie about that!" Cindy's eyes blazed. "That's more their style. Or maybe it was one of Maria's crazy students." She turned looked at me and actually pointed a finger at me! "Ask her about them, Booth always gave her the worst kids! They are everywhere in the building, sneaking around, always saying they are on play business. Seriously, Maria, how could you stand it? Why didn't you have more control over them?"

My mouth dropped open. Smith kicked me under the table. She whispered, "Say nothing."

Cindy didn't even seem to take a breath and continued. "Those kids know everything. And Dickie told Booth everything he heard on his walks around the rooms. And Bill was another one who was always outside of people's doors when he was free. Ask him what he heard."

"I will, but this is about what *you* know." Viola reminded her.

"Okay, I know that Booth defended Dickie all the time. I am sure someone told you about the riot in my room. There was an honest-to-God fist fight! I ended up with a black eye and Booth did nothing! Yes, that's when I said I would kill her, but it was out of frustration. I was sick of her just never doing anything but blame me! Bill was always interested in improving his situation; you should check with the senior girls. All Bill wants is an easier job and a lot of young girls around him. I hear one or two of his female students went to Booth and complained about his friendly ways. Bill would sneak to her with information too. He was always trying to dig his way out of trouble. As for me, I am in the process of applying for a transfer out of here. Booth knew that and she hated me for it. She thought I should stay. She told me she would not have me talking about conditions in this school to another principal. I think she was afraid the state would investigate the school if I said anything about the fight. I wanted out after the fight. I wanted a transfer. But I certainly would not kill her for that."

Cindy stood. And without another word, she walked out of the room.

I was floored. I didn't know what to think. Before anyone could comment there was a knock on the door.

"Come in," said Viola. And in walked Bob, of all people!

"Hi, Detective. I have a few things I want to say."

Viola simply nodded.

Bob went on, "Maria and I talked, but this has been really bothering me. When I spoke to Booth she talked about retiring and other people retiring with her. She laughed about that. She thought she could somehow force some teachers out of the school into early retirement. Now, I have pulled all the faculty files, and no one is really at early retirement age, except Maria and myself. This means a person must have twenty-five years of teaching and be over fifty-five years old. I think Booth was planning something ugly. I mean, she was not really going to retire, except for the fact that she mentioned she had gotten a ton of money, but from whom and for what? Booth enjoyed making everyone's life miserable too much to retire. What was she planning to do? Who was she planning to ruin? Who was paying her off and for what, exactly? I think these are things you should look into."

Smith was writing furiously in her notebook. Viola looked up from his. I just looked at Bob. Who would have guessed that Bob would come into the room with such a good list of questions? Did Bob spend all this time thinking about questions for Viola? Was Bob hiding something?

Viola was quietly taking this all in. "Listen Bob, I really do appreciate all the information. Let's get back to you for a minute. Why did you stay and not transfer out, when there is an assistant principal shortage in the system? I called the Department of Education and they checked for me. You were highly rated every year and could have transferred to a better school. Booth was constantly in your face, so why didn't you do that?"

I was floored. Bob always gave the impression that his ratings were bad.

Bob shrugged. He glanced down at the table. "She really didn't bother me. This school is 15 minutes from my home. And I love the kids. I got to handpick my faculty when they started, and who knows who I would get at another school? Yep, Booth could be a pain, but a new faculty in a new school with new kids could be a pain too. I guess I just got lazy."

Lazy? Bob was never lazy. His meetings were very organized and he was on top of all the teachers' work.

"If you had to guess, who do you think Booth was threatening?"

"I would look at Candy, Bill, Cindy and maybe Dickie, the fair-haired boy."

Viola jumped. "Why Dickie?"

"One day Bill came by my office and said he heard Booth and Dickie yelling at each other in the hallway between classes. I asked what it was about, but he wouldn't say. Maybe you should check with Dickie or Bill. But the thing to remember about Bill is that he makes things up sometimes. I've caught him at it. I have also caught him listening in doorways." They stood, and Viola shook Bob's hand.

"Thank you for coming by," said Viola.

Then he went to the door and looked out into the outer office and waved in Candy. Dickie was with her, but Viola blocked him at the doorway.

"No, I'd like to see her alone." Dickie started to say something, but Viola closed the door firmly.

Candy stood at a chair where Smith had placed her. Her mouth opened in an "oh" as Dickie was pushed out the door by Viola. She sat. She did not look composed.

She then noticed me and glared.

"*WHAT'S SHE DOING HERE?*"

Viola answered. "Mrs. Bruno is helping us with our enquiries. So please tell us what you thought of Mrs. Booth."

"She was Ok to me." Candy smiled at Viola and, I swear, fluttered her eyes.

"Ok? How?"

"Well, she worked on the grant with me and we got a ton of money for my dance classes. She could have just let me do the application myself, but she helped me fill it out correctly, and she called downtown to use her friends to get me funding. We have a great dance program because of that money."

"How much money?"

"$100,000."

"And who kept the records on that money?"

"Booth did and I did." Candy made an ugly face as the thought hit her. "Why? Are you accusing me of something?"

Viola went back to writing in his notebook. He did not look up at her. "Why? Should I be accusing you of something?"

Candy rose from her chair and stormed out of the room without saying another word.

I was shocked. The faculty had talked in little whispers about how remarkable it was that Candy got all that money, when the English Department had been using the same crumbling paperback books for the past 15 years. But no one found out how she managed it. Two English teachers and Bob had gone to the office to see Booth when the grant money was released and asked for new English books. She laughed them out of the office. Bob told us all this in an English faculty meeting. But no one ever learned how Candy got the grant and …why Candy?

I had been hoping that Viola would find out that in this interview, but that was not where he seemed to be headed. He was more interested in where the money was, or where it had gone. Why was he interested? Had something turned up in the accounts? Who could I ask? Oh yes, Sheila Moore, Booth's secretary. Smith and Viola were not talking. Viola glanced at Smith. Smith walked to the door. She asked for Dickie next.

Dickie came in. His walkie-talkie shrieked as he sat down; he did not lower the volume. He looked like a model for a GQ ad as he always did, very well dressed and groomed. But he also looked angry especially when he glanced at Viola. Is that what Viola gets for upsetting Candy? I wondered if she cried when she saw Dickie outside.

Viola looked up. "Tell me, what do you know about the $100,000 dance grant?"

Dickie's face went from red to white. "Not much."

Why was he so suddenly pale?

"Go on."

"I know that the money was used for dance materials for Candy's classes and that Mrs. Booth worked with her on the writing the grant."

Viola waited and said nothing. Dickie stared at him. He looked very nervous and started talking fast.

"I know that they wanted to build a great dance program. The faculty should be proud of Candy and Mrs. Booth for being so interested in the Arts." Dickie started to sweat. "The whole faculty should be thankful to Candy for building such a fine program. The dance program is excellent. You'd have to ask Candy, but I think six kids got dance scholarships to college this year. We should all be proud." Dickie kept sweating and stopped talking.

"What about your job security? What did Booth think of you?"

"Booth was like a mother to me. She was my mother's best friend. She was always very kind to me. I did my job and Booth respected that."

I tried not to laugh out loud. Dickie was never known for doing his job. I could not keep a straight face. I coughed, "sorry."

"Is there any truth to rumor that you and Candy are more than friends?" asked Viola.

"No."

Viola just looked at him.

"No!" said Dickie, "that's not true! We dated once or twice before I got married, but that is all!"

"Ok, Ok, no need to get so hot. Did you and Booth have an argument? "

"No."

"It was overheard."

"By who? Who is listening at doors again? Bill?"

Viola looked at Dickie like he was a bug.

"Yeah, Ok, we argued. She wanted to keep me away from Candy, to not even be Candy's friend." He leered. "I said no and we had an argument about it. I hate school rumors!" He got up and walked out, slamming the door.

Viola smiled at his back. "Smith, let's order lunch. Maria, what are you having?"

I asked for a Cobb salad. Smith took Viola's order and left to go to a local diner. Viola and I looked at each other. "Well, what do you think?" he asked.

"I think we should find out exactly who was stealing funds and where they were putting them. Booth may have been blackmailing someone, but who and why? I don't know. I think Candy is having an affair, but with whom I don't know. And is it important to the murders? Why was Booth murdered? Was it over money? And why kill Roberto? What exactly did he know? Are other students in danger too? I guess this is what's bothering me."

"I agree we need more information. Maybe our next few teachers will give us some more answers."

That's it? That's all he is going to share? Why am I here anyway? I opened my mouth to ask why, when lunch arrived. That ended our first sharing session. Lunch was good though.

Thirty minutes later, I was staring at the Nut Squad. They came in as a group. Jeff was leading the way, with his guitar in hand. The kids were humming some tune softly as they came in. Viola had a strange unnerved look on his face as they filled the room, filling all the chairs and leaned against the walls. He was not used to teenagers and looked almost a bit panicky. He glanced at me for support.

Jeff spoke up. "Hey, detective guy. We went to Roberto's boys. Martha she was Roberto's girl. She took us. His boys claim they had nothing to do with Roberto dying. They seem to have been locked in the county jail for drug dealing at the time he was killed. Them boys are out on bail now."

Jeff smiled at me. "See teach, I told ya I would find out for ya. Detective man, I would look at Ms. Candy and Mr. Dickie if I were you. We've all seen them coming in and out of the kids' locker rooms together at night and early morning. They seemed very tight, if you know what I mean." Jeff winked at Viola.

Martha spoke up with a Kleenex in her hand. "Yes, they tried to tell us they were doing locker checks to see if we were stashing drugs there. But you'd have to be a stupid kid to hide drugs in your gym locker, when there are lots of better places to hide 'em at school. Lots of better places." She turned red. Jeff jumped in.

"Yeah, I mean we may be dummies, but we ain't *that dumb*, Teach, Detective," he nodded his head snapped his fingers. The others walked out in a group following his lead. As the last one went out the door, and I had just started to take a breath, Jeff stuck his head back in. "We are on it Teach." He nodded and winked at me. I smiled weakly at him. And this time, he left for good.

Viola was totally red faced. "Well Maria, some group you have there. I may have to bring additional forces into the school to look for nice places to hide drugs. But for now, I want to concentrate on the murders. If Roberto's gang was locked up, that leaves them out. Smith, check that for me. Also, Maria, what exactly are they on? What did they mean?"

I crossed my fingers under the table, looked Viola dead in the eye, and told him I had no idea.

"On it, Chief" said Smith. She pulled out a cellphone and walked into the hallway to make her call.

We were alone. He smiled at me. I felt my heart float. His smile could do that to me even after all these years. Would I ever get over Viola? He was as handsome as our first date. I wish he had told me why we could not get married. When he spoke, it broke my off my thoughts of the past.

"So, Maria, who do you think I should talk to next, since we met your students?"

I smiled back. I may be married, but I am not dead. I could still flirt. "I would try the custodians or the secretaries. They know everything in the school, after the students. Bill said yesterday he was working on learning something more for me, so I think…" That's as far as I got. Viola looked strangely angry. Why did he look like that?

"What do you mean you talked to him yesterday? I told you this is murder and dangerous! Maria, I don't want you checking on people."

Well, he did not tell me not to snoop around. Smith did.

Now I was getting upset too. "I know, but I want to help. I'm afraid my students could be in danger after what happened to Roberto. I know

71

the school and the students and faculty better than you do!"

"I realize that you know everyone better," he said, very loudly now, "but I don't want you hurt!"

I was about to make a curt reply, but enter Smith, with worry lines on her face, from our discussion no doubt. Viola and I both turned red-faced to look at her. We both took a deep breath. She glanced from me to Joe and back with concern. We sat and glared her.

She coughed. "I checked with the jail. The students were right, Roberto's gang was in jail for a rock throwing incident at the local drug store. They may have been trying to break in to get free drugs. Bail was posted by a group of their parents the next day, so for the time of Roberto's murder they are in the clear."

"Ok, said Viola, "I am going to walk Maria to her car. It's the end of the day. Tomorrow we'll interview the office staff and any teachers we've missed. "

I liked the "we" in the sentence. Maybe I was included?

We walked to the car in silence. As I touched the car door handle, Joe grabbed my hand. "Maria, this is not an academic puzzle. You must be careful." He held the door with his other hand.

I looked at his hand holding mine. His face turned red and he let go. I turned, got into the car and said, "I will." He shut the door. I went home.

14

The Second Day in the Interview Room

The next day was cloudy and rainy, like my mood. I set up a substitute teacher for my classes using the school hotline for teachers. I had tons of sick days accumulated over the years. I wanted to keep hunting with Viola. I knew I should get to Booth's office staff today, but once again I headed for the conference room and Viola.

Smith was already there. She handed me a cup of coffee as I came in. Viola had stacks of paper in front of him, which he seemed to be reading. Little did he know I was not going to bother him after yesterday's little tiff. The handholding had confused me to death. Was he interested in me after all these years, or was I imagining it? I really did not want to think about it. And I certainly was not going to think about his warning that I could be hurt.

Someone had left Booth's dead body for me to discover, someone knew I was always on time for my meetings with her. Heck, the whole staff knew that I was never late for anything. And the meetings were posted in the weekly newsletter in advance, so everyone knew. The killer had set up the murder to coincide with my appointment with Booth.

Also, Roberto's death really made me mad. He was not a brilliant student, his Hamlet would have made a *New York Times* critic pass out in his seat, but he was my student. He did not deserve to be murdered on my stage! Someone was making me mad. Someone had to be exposed and no one was going to stop me, at least not the way I felt today.

Viola looked up from his papers. What he had been reading? He nodded to Smith. "Let's have Marge, the English teacher, in next."

Smith went out. Why Marge? I wondered to myself? She was not the brightest egg, even though the kids loved her for her easy grades. She told me the first year we taught together that Master Plots were the only thing she used. She never really read a high school book.

Smith and Marge came in. Marge sat down.

"Marge," said Viola, "How did Booth treat you?"

Marge smiled. "She hated me for being such an easy grader and well-liked by the students. But I do not believe in punishing growing minds. We had many discussions after she saw my lessons regarding this and the lack of rules in my room. I believe in student-driven curriculum, even if it is not the same as the standards. She did not like this, but I have tenure so what could she do? Besides the kids would have not liked it if she had gotten rid of me. They really love me. If you are asking if I killed her, the answer is no."

That may be true I thought. But they really love your grades.

Viola frowned at her. Marge sat and did not change her facial expression as she stared back.

"Did she try to get rid of you?" he asked.

Marge shifted slightly in the chair. "She may have wanted to, but besides her pointing out every little thing she did not like in the conference room when we went over my lessons, I don't think she was working on getting rid of me. She was working on making others miserable, like Bill and maybe, Candy or Cindy. You should speak to them."

"Why?"

Marge stared at Viola. "I can't believe no one has told you." She glanced at me. "Cindy was in trouble for the fight in her room, and trying to pin it on Booth's favorite, Dickie. Candy was in trouble for dating Dickie and Bill. Bill was in trouble because his senior girls complained about him and his hands-on policy." She had bigger fish to fry than me. Besides the parents were happy with me. I passed almost everyone." She stopped. "Anything else?"

"No" said Viola.

Marge got up and left.

Bill Mecca walked in when Marge left. He sank into a chair and straightened out his Italian pants and jacket. He looked Italian for the Italian classes and he dressed Italian. He was still slim, with thick brown hair, which had to be dyed at his age and fell at times into his dreamy dark brown eyes. No wonder the girls loved him. He was the perfect teenage idol. Viola smiled at him, a nice toothy smile. Bill smiled back.

"So," said Viola, "what can you tell me about your relationship with Booth?"

"Booth was Ok to me. We got along well."

"What is this I hear about you and the senior girls?"

"Ah, senior girls, they have big imaginations, right? Booth thought that since they came to her and complained that I was being too sexy with them, there was some kind of problem. What a joke! I know what I look like and I am very cautious not to be alone with any girl. Not that some of them haven't asked…." he smiled widely.

He really made me sick.

Viola waited.

"But nothing has ever happened. Even though people think so. I am very careful in and out of school. I can't help it if senior girls like to follow me around. This is what I explained to Booth. And she understood."

"Did she understand about Candy?"

Bill laughed. "Candy is a grown woman. If, and I am only saying if, we dated, then what could Booth say? Nothing. But I want to tell you about something my senior girls said. They have said that Roberto was known for listening at classroom doors and talking about what he heard. Perhaps you should follow up on that, and not worry about me so much." He stood. "May I leave?" and without waiting for permission, he walked out.

"Well!" said Smith as she rose to go after Bill. Viola waved her back down.

"So," asked Viola, looking at me directly for the first time all morning, "what do you think?"

"Personally, I find it amazing that Bill admitted two things; one, that he was seeing Candy, and two, that he had these strange relationships with senior girls. I think he was in a lot of trouble about that with Booth, no matter what he says."

"I agree. But what do you think that has to do with Booth's or Roberto's murder? He could have been asked to resign, but is that reason enough to kill two people? And, why kill Roberto? It just doesn't add up. Let's hear from Sheila Moore next. I still think it has something to do with the grant funds."

"Sheila Moore will be a tough nut to crack. She believed in Booth and was a strong backer of her rules and regulations."

"We will see."

Sheila came in wearing a grey suit. She always wore suits in very uninteresting colors. She was tall, about 5 feet, 10 inches. Her grey hair was pulled off her face in a ponytail. She wore lipstick and no other makeup. She sat down in the chair with ramrod stiffness.

"Well, Ms. Moore, what exactly was Mrs. Booth like?" asked Viola.

"What do you mean?"

"I mean, what type of person was she to work for? Easygoing?"   .

Then a strange thing happened. Sheila started to laugh. And this was a sound I had never heard before. I am sure no faculty member had ever heard Sheila laugh. I stared and felt chills run up and down my spine. Was Sheila cracking up? It took a minute or so for Sheila to stop laughing.

"Easygoing? No, she was not easygoing. She was a demanding, hard person. She wanted everything to be correct the first time. She was impossible to work for but I put up with her to keep my job. And if it was not correct, she could be nasty. She was hard on her staff. But she knew how to run a school efficiently. Her test scores were decent. I am sure many of the teachers have told you she did not like them. They shouldn't feel badly; she did not like anyone. She was a user. But for all of that, she ran a good school."

"Did you like her?"

"No, but I respected her position." Sheila stopped, licked her lips and said no more.

"Do you keep the accounts for her budgets?"

"Yes, I do, except the grants. She kept her own grant records."

"Why?"

"Why? I don't know the answer Ok? She would not let me keep them."

"Have you any idea why?"

"No," said Sheila with a smile, "you would have to ask her."

She grinned.

Viola looked at her strangely. We were all looking at her strangely. In twenty years, this was a woman I had never seen smile in her office. But she was smiling now. Was Sheila happy to be rid of Booth? It sure looked that way.

"But if you are interested in the grants," said Sheila, "I suggest Candy would know. Or maybe Dickie or Bill; either one of them should know. If not, I guess Booth was the only one to know. You can check her desk computer or her files. I don't even have a password for her computer, so there must be something interesting on it. She never let me use it." Sheila smiled again.

"Thank you, Ms. Moore," said Viola. "You can go."

Sheila walked out of the room still smiling.

I'd have thought Sheila would have been very upset about Booth's demise. She was always on Booth's side in when it came to office politics. You never heard her say a word against her principal. Who knew that she really did not like Booth?

Viola turned to Smith. "Well," he said, "you're the computer person. I guess you should go to Booth's office and see what you can find out from her computer. I'll take notes here for us both."

Smith stood and said, "Aye, aye, Captain." And she was out the door.

Viola looked at me. I looked at him. "What did you think?" he asked.

"I think Sheila is a very strange woman, one we all thought was a Booth clone. But, I guess we were all wrong."

"I guess you were. But do you think she could have killed Booth?"

For a second, I was shocked. For the past few minutes, I had been thinking of this as a puzzle and had almost forgotten that two people were dead. With my student and Booth both murdered, it was time to really think about the people I knew who could have killed them. Could Sheila be a murderer? She was tall and strong. But could she kill Booth? Why would she kill Booth? And who would kill Roberto? Ok, he was not the best student, and he did talk too much, and never learned lines, but why would someone kill him? Could Sheila have killed him?

"Joe, I don't know why Sheila would kill Booth or Roberto. We have to find a reason, a motive."

"Yes, that's the trick, isn't it? Why were they killed? If we can find the why, that may lead us to the who. But do you think Sheila could kill?"

"I suppose anyone could kill. If you are asking me is Sheila strong enough, I would say yes, but why? And why kill Roberto?"

"Maybe Booth threatened to fire her?"

"Ok, but Sheila is a union member and a very good secretary. Principals who visit here love her; she is very organized and types over 100 words a minute. She could get a job in another school in five minutes. So that can't be a reason."

"Could Booth have known something about her that she did not want anyone to know?"

"Like what?"

"An affair with someone, or missing funds?"

"It's possible, but the woman lives with her mother, and I have never heard a rumor about her in the school. As far as missing funds, she said she didn't work with the grants. And the grants are where the extra money is. So, if you want to steal money from a school, grants are the best way, but Booth kept tight control and her own grant records."

"That's true, Maria, if we believe Sheila."

"Yes," I said slowly, "if we believe Sheila..."

The dismissal bell rang. Viola walked me to my car. Neither one of us spoke. We were both thinking about what we had heard today. I got in my car and drove home.

15

Interview Day 3 When in Doubt; Ask the Guys Who Sweep Your Floor

Before I left home for school. I spoke to Tommie and asked him to call a substitute for me for the day. He had no problem with this as he wanted the murders solved. The custodians and I arrived at the Interview Room together. I sat in

my seat and Viola waved Rich and Nat to their
chairs.

Nat spoke first, even before Viola looked up
from his notebook. "There have been some
strange things going in our office in the
basement. Furniture has been moved. Desks have
been moved. We keep our office locked, so that
means someone else has keys. There are supplies
missing from the closets, like stuff to clean floors
and clean cement and also to start fires. The
boiler seems to be low on fuel a lot. I spoke to
Booth about it. I don't know if she did anything.
Maybe she was late paying the gas and oil bills.
Some rags in boxes are missing, too."

He sat back. Viola leaned forward, his face
tense. "Could this stuff that is missing have been
used to create a bomb?"

Nat frowned and turned to Rich. Rich spoke
for the first time. "Gee, I don't know, what type
of crazy person would want to do that?"

Viola replied. "The same kind of crazy person
who has killed two people. I am sending you both
with an officer to the basement. Spend the rest of
the day checking to see what exactly is missing
and give the officer a list." Viola jumped up,
walked to the door and called to one of the
uniformed officers. He explained exactly what
he wanted, and sent the three of them to the
basement.

I felt chills running through my body. If there
was a bomb, where in the building would it be?
Who was really this crazy? The auditorium was

huge and so was the backstage area. That would make a perfect hiding place. I stood. Viola stared at me. "Maria, where are you going?"

"I want to check backstage."

Viola sighed. "First of all, my officers were all over that area when Roberto was killed. We would have noticed a bomb. Second, until I know what is missing, we can't even say a bomb could have been created. We have to wait to see what is missing. And both the murders have been against individuals, not a group of people, which if you were making a bomb is what you would want to target. "

"Yes, that is true," I said, "but what if the murderer is getting crazier?"

"He or she could be, but Maria it is quite a step from murderer to bomber. Let's wait and see exactly what's missing, before we start running around the building?"

"Ok." I sat back down.

Viola drummed his pen on the tabletop. I gazed out the window. The dismissal bell rang. We waited in silence. I was thought hard about who could feel so angry or so scared of Booth that they felt she had to die. Many a school hated their principal, but that did not mean a faculty member would really be moved to kill one. They might think about it, even joke about it in the faculty room, but, honestly, plot to do it? Faculty members in all schools had problems.

One could understand someone so angry they would kill the principal, but would they also kill a student? Yeah, we all joked about killing the odd student now and then, but to really do it because they overheard or knew something, I could not imagine. I was very angry about Roberto's death. Who in their right mind would kill a student? And why were there no clues? No fingerprints? No hair at the scenes? This was very well planned. Why kill my student? Did that mean anything? Was I closer to the killer than I suspected? I turned to Viola, who was staring at the tabletop and still tapping his pen. I coughed. He looked at me.

"Why my student? Why Roberto? Anyone could have properly paid him off with a bribe of some kind if he had overheard anything. He loved electronics and candy. Why go to the extreme of killing him? A smart teacher could have convinced him that what he overheard was not true, or part of a script, or a hundred different things. Why kill him? Was it because he was one of *my* students?"

Viola starred at me for a minute. "Tonight, when you go home, seriously think about whether there is anything you know that you have not shared with me. I don't think Roberto was killed because of his relationship with you. I think he was killed because whatever Roberto heard outside the rooms put the killer in danger. Or he could have been killed because of something he knew and shared about Booth, and they were both killed for the same reason. The third possibility is that you know something, and killing Roberto was a warning for you to stay out of hunting for the killer. If that is true, you should stay away from this situation all together."

Someone knocked. The officer and the custodians filed in. The officer handed Viola a few pieces of paper and walked out. The custodians sat down. Viola looked at the paper and then he spoke. "There seems to be a lot of stuff missing, which means I have to have police come here again to search the building for the components to make fires or bombs. I want you to change your office keys today. Use keys from outside the building, not keys that were used here before. That's all for now." Viola got up and walked to the principal's office door. He did not even knock. He told Tommy Newbie to evacuate the building immediately. He then found Smith at Booth's computer and told her she was in charge of an immediate building search. The dismissal bell had already rung, so sports were the only activities still in place in the building. The principal ordered an evacuation announcement over the loudspeaker. "Get everyone out now!"

Hey, so nice to remain calm and not scare everyone.

Smith grabbed her cellphone and called for backup. The principal grabbed his computer and pushed past me for the nearest exit. Another sterling example of leadership, I thought. Principals out of the building before all the teachers and students.

As Tommy Newbie pushed past without a word, Viola held my arm to help me keep my balance. He said, "I am walking you to your car." Smith came out of the office at a jog. "I can walk Maria to her car. sir, as I have to stand outside to direct the arriving police. You should get your notes out of here and, if you would not mind, grab Booth's computer, just in case."

"Good idea, Smith, Maria see you here in the morning." Viola gave me a full volt smile and a wave and jogged back into the building. I wearily waved back. What else could happen? Would the school explode? I noticed that Candy and Dickie and a lot of kids in gym clothes were on the track at the far end away from the school. The newbie principal was there too, so maybe he was not so bad. I had thought he was running for his car when he left.

16

Is that a Bomb I See Before Me?

Smith and I got to my car. Smith opened the door. "Maria, you should really lock your car."

"You're right. I forgot this morning."

I turned on the ignition, and nothing happened. Great! Now the car was dead. I have to call AAA and wait for them to show up. I went to turn on the ignition again, but Smith grabbed my hand.

Her eyes had gone wide with fear. "Get out now! Now Maria!" I moved quicker than I had in twenty years.

We ran about 20 feet and then the car exploded in a red ball of fire. Smith jumped on top of me and threw us to the shaking ground. Car parts flew over us both. That is all I remember, until I woke up in the hospital and Al was sitting next to my white hospital bed holding my hand. I was happy to be holding Al's hand, he was my rock. But then why was I thinking about Viola?

"Hi", I said weakly, my voice sounding like it was coming from a deep hole in the ground. Boy, did my head hurt! I reached for my head and as I did Al grabbed my free hand.

"Hold on there," he said, "let me tell you what happened."

"You have a bandage on your head; and a cut near your hairline. They think you have a concussion, and you may have an ear problem for a few days. You have bruises and minor cuts in lots of places. Some of your clothes were on fire. You have a few burns but nothing serious. They said you could come home tomorrow after they check you out for your head injury. Maria, you were very lucky. I am very afraid." He paused and looked into my eyes. "Whatever you are doing, playing detective, it has to stop. Promise me it will stop now. Someone is out to kill you."

I crossed my fingers under the sheet and promised him. He looked very worried, but I was not about to stop looking for Roberto's killer, one way or another. Especially since I now knew I was not going to die, at least not today. Then I remembered Officer Smith. "How is Smith?"

Al sighed. I think in his heart of hearts he knew nothing would stop me. He knew he had married a very stubborn short Italian lady. "Well, Smith is another story. Since she covered you with her body, she was hit in the head by car parts." I flinched. "They put her in a coma to reduce the swelling on her brain and hope she will recover. Besides the head injury she was not hurt. Viola is with her now. He's quite upset. She is only 24 and he had to call her parents, who are flying in from California. You were both lucky that you ran before the explosion, or you could have been killed." He leaned over and kissed me. "Viola wanted to know when you woke up. I'll go find him. But Maria, I really want this to stop now."

He shook his head and walked out the door. I watched him go, standing tall, with his beautiful curly silver hair. We both knew that our students were like the children we had never had. We were very protective of them. He knew how angry I was about Roberto. And I knew that if our situation were reversed, he would do all he could to find the killer too. I leaned back and closed my eyes. When I woke up, Viola was sitting by my bed. Al was sitting in the chair against the wall, arms crossed. He stared at Viola, not blinking. What body language! These two boys didn't really like each other.

Viola spoke. "Maria, I am so sorry. Go home tomorrow and get some rest. Al said he doesn't want you involved anymore and I agree."

I nodded which made my head hurt but said nothing. I am not about to protest with a committee of naysayers in the room. I am smarter than that.

Viola continued, "There is no school tomorrow anyway. The principal has hired counselors to talk to the students. The parents are upset. You have to think of yourself. This bomb was meant for one person, you. Think about what you know and tell me if you remember anything you did not tell me before. Call me." He got up to go. He took my hand. 'Be well." He started for the door. Al rose, maybe to make sure he left.

"Wait a minute," I said. "How is Smith?"

Viola turned with the doorknob in his manly hand. "Smith is still in a coma, but her foot moved today, so they hope she will wake up soon. I am going there now to sit with her parents."

"She saved my life. She threw herself on top of me. I wouldn't be alive now without Smith. Tell her parents as soon as they let me out of this bed, I want to stop by and see her."

"I'll tell them."

And he left. Al came over and kissed me goodnight. He was going home to rest. I told him I was fine and would see him in the morning. I was glad he was leaving, as I had a lot to think about.

I couldn't think with the bruises, and I just fell asleep. When I woke up the next morning a doctor was by my bed. He was brown haired and about 30 and very cute. He smiled when I woke up. "Hi, Maria, you have a slight concussion, your hearing maybe be off for a few days, but it will return. The bruises and burns are minor. You were very lucky. After breakfast today, you can go home and rest." He quickly walked out the door. Rats! I did not even get the cute doctor's name.

Al came and got me after breakfast. We went down the hall and met Smith's parents. Smith looked very small for such a big girl in the hospital bed. She was still not awake. Her Mom looked like she had been crying when we came in. She was holding Smith's big hand in hers. I hoped Smith would wake up soon. I exchanged numbers with her parents, and I told them how brave Smith had been to save me. They were very nice people. It was all very upsetting.

We went home. I limped into our apartment and went to lay down on the couch. I tried to follow Viola's instructions and really think. You know how in murder mystery books the answer jumps out at the heroine? Well, don't believe it. It was not happening to me.

Bob my assistant principal, called, to see how I was doing. I started to ask him why he hadn't told anyone that he really got along with Principal Booth, but he said he had to go and hung up on me! Viola called. He said that Smith, thank goodness, was awake and would be released in a few days. She was going to California with her parents to recover and was off the case and on medical leave from the police department. I began to pace around the apartment, hoping something would jump out at me as a clue. Al hovered, offering me drinks and staring into my face as if I were sick. It was great that someone from his fish club called. They had a tropical fish emergency, so he had to go. He was a fish doctor for the club! I told him I would be fine. As soon as the door closed, I wrote him a note saying I had left something important at school and would be right back. I dressed, called a taxi and went to school. Something about the custodian offices struck me as fishy. I was not sure what. But I wanted to look.

17

"By the Pricking on My Thumbs,
Something Wicked This Way Comes." (Macbeth)

When I got to the school, it was after four o'clock, and only a few if any people would be in the building. Good, I didn't want anyone to know what I was planning to do. I had a key because of the school play. The halls were ghostly without students though I heard footsteps above me on the second floor. I walked the first floor to the basement entrance. I climbed down the stairs to the basement, my sneakers making no sound on the stairs. As I opened the basement door, I got a strange feeling that someone was following me. I stopped as I opened the door, turned around and saw and heard nothing. Silently, I walked to the custodian room. As I arrived there, I remembered that Viola had told them to change the locks Oh boy, was I slow! I decided to try the door anyway. Oddly enough it was open. I stood in the doorway looking into the office. It was a mess, papers and supplies everywhere, paint on the floor running toward the windows. Did the Department of Education ever make an even floor? Then it hit me. This was not damage from a police search. This was someone looking for something. Suddenly I wondered if what they were looking for was bomb parts. A chill went up my spine. Then the lights in the basement went out.

Now I was scared and knew I was not alone here. There was very little light. The windows in parts of the basement were half windows; they were not big enough to let me crawl out. I realized I would be trapped if I stayed in this room, I would have more luck in the hallway, where there were stairs to the first floor and exits from the building. There were two stairways so a lone killer could not be guarding both of them at the same time. I tiptoed out into the hall and heard nothing. Slowly I moved to the first and closest stairway to the right. The lights were out, but the high windows were letting in the setting sunlight. It was enough light to see by. Then I heard the click of a lock turning on the stairway door to the first floor. Someone had locked the basement door on this exit. All doors in the school had keys, but the basement doors were never locked, due to the possibility of fire. I mean, who would want a custodian to burn up? The light in the stairway was very dim; all I could see was a strange, tall, lumpy shape at the top of the stairs. The shape moved slightly. I quickly and quietly reversed direction and headed for the stairway at the other end of the hall.

Then the whispering started. "Maria, Maria," it whispered. I couldn't tell if it was a man or a woman, the voice was high and light in back of me. I kept moving as swiftly and silently as I could to the other stairway. Now I wished I had joined Candy on those track runs.

"Maria, Maria," it whispered again. I made a vow then and there, if I survived tonight, I would go to the gym three days a week. "Maria, you should leave this case alone. The bomb didn't stop you," it whispered, "but I can." I moved even faster for the other exit.

Then I heard whoosh. Something brushed my head. I glanced down the hall to the place it had landed. A can of the industrial green paint used in all schools slapped down the hall ahead of me. If that had hit me, I would be unconscious for sure. I reached the stairway and I screamed as loudly as I could as I sped up the stairs. The murderer was throwing full paint cans at me to knock me down! I got to the top of the stairs. The door was locked. I pounded on it. The murderer had probably locked it first. I knew then that I was a dead duck. I screamed again, but I knew no one was in the building this late. A strange thought hit me: Al is going to kill me if I get murdered!

The shadowy person started walking up the stairs. Suddenly the door that I was pounding on in terror, opened. I fell at the person's feet. I would have known those Gucci's anywhere. It was Viola. "Hurry! The murderer is in the basement!" I gasped out. He stepped over me quickly, did not even offer me a hand off the floor, and is gallantry dead? I guessed so. He raced down the steps at a dead run. Well, I thought, at least one of us goes to the gym. Then I remembered the promise I had made to myself and groaned. Three days a week in the gym! I would die.

I sat up. Then I slowly got to my feet, staying by the door. What I had been thinking? Why did I think I could find a clue in the basement? Did I think I was Nancy Drew? Was I crazy? Whoever was in the basement wanted to kill me. I would not be able to stop a maniac. But I wanted to know immediately if Viola caught him or her.

Finally, I heard steps across the basement floor. They started up the stairs. I stared down the dark staircase. I took the fire extinguisher off the wall just in case I needed it as a weapon.

"It's me," Viola said, as he climbed up the stairs slowly. I put the fire extinguisher back. "I ran but it was too fast. It was wearing some kind of flowing dark cape. You couldn't even tell if it was a man or woman. And I nearly broke my neck slipping on some paint."

He came into the light on the first floor. Here were big windows, floor to ceiling windows. At least in the dusk, you could see. One side of Viola's nice designer suit and part of his hair and face were covered in green industrial paint. He was lucky his grandparents had left him a small trust. He had told me, while we were engaged, that he used that money to buy his clothes. Maybe I should have mentioned that the murderer had thrown paint cans at me before I sent Viola down the stairs? But I was just grateful to be out of the basement! Really, who can think of everything?

Viola brushed past me, pulled out his cellphone and ordered all police who were guarding the outside of the school, to come in and do a building search. He then grabbed me by the arm and frog-marched me out of the building. We sat on a bench by the front door of the school. It faced an exit door, I guess in case the murderer decided to come our way. But, in my heart I knew it was useless. That person in the basement was long gone. There were at least 14 exits to the building, and the murderer knew the building like I did.

With a school population of four thousand there had to be a lot of exits. My phone rang. It was Al. He yelled at me. Viola and half the building could have heard it. He was very angry that I had gone back to school. I told him I was with Viola.

I handed Viola the phone. He said that for some reason not yet explained to him, I had gone to the basement. He then told Al I had met the killer. The killer had chased me in the basement. No, I was all right. Viola would bring me home as soon as he got a statement from me.

They both agreed that I was impossible. When I heard Viola tell Al that he should take my wallet away, so I did not have money to return to school, that was too much. I grabbed back the phone. I told Al he better not try it, and that I was Ok, and would be home soon. I ended the phone call. Viola, still wearing green paint on one side of his face, glared at me. I glared back. For a second, he reminded me of the Incredible Hulk.

"What happened? Tell me exactly what happened and explain why you were in the basement." He paused and then added, "Please." Well, the "please" did it. Viola was really getting on my nerves. How could I explain that something about the custodian interview bothered me? The custodians never were very helpful in the school. Why would they keep flammable objects around? And the key discussion bothered me. Custodians are the guys who have all the keys. Slowly I started to speak.

"Something about the custodians' story bothered me. Don't ask what, because I don't know exactly, maybe it was the break-ins. The custodians have most of the keys to the whole building usually, so how did someone else get keys? Were the keys stolen from the custodians? Anyway, I had an odd feeling about the whole thing and I came back.

Maybe the car bombing rattled my brains, and I am not thinking straight. Or maybe I think a lot like this killer. I am a teacher, and I think our killer is a teacher too, not a staff member. Staff people leave the building later; a few of them might know my car, but not all of them. Teachers ride with teachers all the time, to lunches, meetings, free trips home, for people who don't have cars. It makes sense that it is a teacher.

Also, if you were looking for something in the custodians' office, why not just look? Why trash the office? These custodians aren't the tidiest people. They might never know you had been there if you were careful. But this person is not careful. I think I know why. The custodians in this building have to be asked four times to do things for teachers. For example, boards are to be cleaned every day. They don't do it. You want your board cleaned, you are better off doing it yourself. These guys are nice but very lazy, and keep in mind, some of them make more than the teachers. This crime I think, has been done by someone who is very mad at the custodial staff. Or by someone who sees the trashing of the office as a way of throwing off the investigation."

"Maybe but explain what happened in the basement."

"I was in the custodial office. The lights went out. Before that, when I walked into the building I heard footsteps above me on the second floor. So, I felt that when the lights went out, I was not alone. It really scared me."

I started to shake. Viola stood took off his suit jacket, with its lovely damp green paint, and wrapped it about my shoulders. It was still warm from his body. It felt good.

"I tried the west stair exit. But whoever was in the building was there, and I could hear the key turn in the lock. I saw a lumpy tall shape on the stairs like a wrapped body. I couldn't see if it was a man or a woman. I could really tell nothing about it. I tried to be quiet and rushed to the exit on the east side of the building, where you found me. It charged after me, but I must have been faster than I thought, or the thing never really wanted to catch me.

It whispered "Maria, Maria" twice, and then it said that since the bomb did not kill me, it would. It told me to stop meddling in the case. The voice could have been a male or female. It was a whisper and high pitched. Then it threw the paint can at me, which barely missed my head. I ran up the stairs and you opened the door. It started up the steps but then I guess it saw you and ran.

I think it ran out the other doorway. It had to have a key. Once it got to the first floor it had a lot of exits to choose from. Heck, if the thing was athletic, it could have gone out one of those long windows; they can all be opened. My taxi was the only car in the lot when I arrived, but people sometimes park on the street, so they can exit the school sooner. It scared me. That's all I know."

My teeth started to chatter. I was so cold and tired. Viola was looking at me as if I was a lab rat. He did not look happy. He sighed. He got on his phone. From his end of the conversation I gathered that the police search had found nothing. I glanced at him as he talked. I suddenly remembered something.

I stood and handed him back his jacket. He stood, hung up the phone and looked at me. I headed back into the school. "Wait a minute!" he said. I stopped.

I turned back to look at him, "The cape, I know where the cape is."

"Maria, tell me where," as he spoke, I could hear him grinding his teeth. "There is a killer loose. I do not want you in the school again."

"Well, if I tell you will you go check?"

"Yes," he said loudly, still angry.

"It's backstage. But I have the keys and you are not leaving me here while you look. I am not sitting here by myself when a killer could come out that door at any minute. I refuse to face the killer again tonight! Besides, I have the keys. You don't."

I never saw a man's face turn quite that shade of red before. He stopped and took a deep breath. His face almost looked normal again; a strange smile appeared. "You are too much. I had forgotten you could be like this. All right, we will look together, but then you are going to go home. Because I am going to drive you there."

"Ok." I agreed. Al was jumping by now; I knew it.

We walked into the building together. The detective pushed me in back of him. He led. I followed. We entered the auditorium together. I turned on the auditorium lights at the back of the seats. The stage was dark but the auditorium was light. I saw a mound on the stage. "Look!" I hissed and pointed.

"Can we get more lights?" he whispered back. I walked to the door of the auditorium and turned the house lights full up. There, downstage center, was what looked like a mound of clothing. I hoped there was no body under there, we both walked slowly onto the stage. Viola held up a hand to stop me from going forward. He appeared to be listening. We both heard nothing.

On the downstage, was a very neat pile of all the cloaks from Hamlet. It looked to be all fifteen of them. I knew how many I had ordered. They were lying on the stage as if someone had arranged them. They had been painted industrial green, and the paint job was not neat at all: in fact, the paint had been poured over every one of them. Most of the downstage area was now industrial New York City Board of Education Green. The stage floor had been a beautiful wooden polished floor. It was ruined. Three empty gallons of paint stood tipped over on their sides next to the clothes.

"Stay here! Don't come near the pile."

He wanted to check to see if there was a body. I did not follow him. Frankly I did not want to see another dead body ever again. He took one of his Gucci-clad feet, and gently kicked the pile till he could see the floor under the cloaks. Those Gucci's were toast.

Thank goodness there was nothing under the cloaks. I started to wonder about the costume rental bills for the ruined cloaks. As I was wondering, he spoke, but not to me. His phone was out again and he was calling for back-up. Two cops in uniform came running down the sides of the auditorium to stand near me. He ordered them to secure the site for photos and fingerprinting. Funny, there were no footprints in the paint. How could anyone pour all that paint over all those cloaks and not leave any footprints? This clearly was a person who planned things out. Viola then looked at me. "Maria, I think this is getting rather personal. Do me a favor please I beg you, and stay home?"

I promised I would. I was not one to resist a begging man. I really had not thought it was personal until the bomb. But I did now. Then, I remembered that Parent's Night was next week. Oh well, I wouldn't tell Viola yet. I hoped Al didn't remember. He might lock me in the apartment after that.

Viola took me home.

Al kissed me firmly. We went to bed.

18

Parents Night or What! Not My Child!

The next few days were normal. I stayed home, and Al and I went out for dinner with friends. Viola did not call, and I did not call. I waited for my favorite day of the year, Parents Night! Each New York City high school teacher has about 160 students in their classes. This is a teacher's one chance to tell parents of brilliant students in three minutes each, that their children are really brilliant. The same three minutes each is for parents of students who are not so brilliant. I was hoping some of the Nut Squad's parents would come. I had tried to reach many of them on the phone, but most of the phone numbers were wrong numbers given to me by the students. This was not a surprise. There is a special club, which gives ideas to students who do not want teacher contact with parents. I secretly find it amazing how much work some students can put into:

1. Cheating on tests using cellphones on their lap.
2. Handing in the same answers on five different students homework assignments when each student was given different questions.

3. Spending time in which they could write the 250-word essay looking up the assignment online at a cheat site and turning it in as if I were too stupid to look online. Or two students writing the same exact essay.
4. Telling parents, I don't give homework, that they don't have class every day, and they have perfect attendance and don't ever cut!

Yes, I really looked forward to Parents Night.

The trick would be getting to go. I finally told Al it was Parents Night, which just happened to fall on his fish club meeting night. So, he had to let me go without him. He was not pleased, but I told him I would call at the end of the evening as I was leaving the school, and yes, I would walk with someone to my car.

I then called Tommie Newbie, the principal, (I really had to learn this guy's name sometime soon) and told his secretary that I would be in for Parents Night. She sounded relieved. This would save the office the job of putting a list on my door for parents to sign that I was not there, and that someone would call them, sometime. I was off to Parent's Night! I wondered if Viola would be there. Did he now know anything that he wanted to share?

I pulled into a full parking lot, but my assigned space was empty. Yes, the ground where I parked was a dark burnt color due to the bomb, but otherwise there was plenty of room. The teachers who usually parked next to me had left their spots empty. No one wanted to park close to me. They were all afraid. No one wanted to share another bomb attack with me.

At least I could easily get in and out of my new car leased by the insurance company. I walked to the front door of the school, past the spotted green and brown colored bench where Viola and I had sat days ago. Ah, memories. Then I got nervous as I entered the lobby. Did he know anything yet about the painted cloaks? Or who this crazy person was?

In the lobby, gathered around the sports trophies and the bulletin boards stood almost all the teachers. They were strangely silent. I wondered why. On Parents Night there is a faculty tradition at our school. The whole staff goes out to a good restaurant together before the event. Many of us are on different schedules, so we don't get to see much of each other during the year. It is fun, but tonight I had not gone. I didn't want to see all of the group together; it made me nervous. I didn't want to have to wonder as I sat eating my dinner, if one of them was a murderer.

Then I saw Viola and Principal Newbie standing close to the bulletin board together. Viola smiled at me and said, "We seem to have a gossip columnist in the school." I looked at the silent group and then Viola pointed to the bulletin board. I eased in front of him and Tommie to read the notice that had been posted. It was a list of times and dates. It gave details of the weather for each day that was listed. It also stated that Candy, Dickie and Bill were having a love affair. This was the reason for the silent group. Viola turned to the principal. "Was everyone at dinner together?"

"Yes, we were all there together."

"No one left to come back to the school early?"

"No, we all came back in a group of cars together, no one rode alone."

"Did the persons mentioned ride together?"

Everyone looked at each other. No one spoke. Finally, Dickie said, "This is slander! It is not true! Yes, Bill, Candy and I rode together to the restaurant, but Megan came with us. We did not stop anywhere for a quickie!" At this point Dickie was angry. His face looked like a ripe tomato.

This was very interesting.

The newbie principal looked like he was ready to blow his top. "All teachers assigned to bulletin boards go around the school now before we open the doors and take this notice down if you see it anywhere." He barked at us, "bring the copies to my office immediately." He turned to Viola. "This is the end. I expect you to solve this!"

Dickie jogged off somewhere, perhaps to find the other two in the threesome and share the good news.

Viola said nothing in reply. Tommie Newbie turned on his heels to get his keys out of his pocket and locked the front doors to stop the parents from coming in before he got the notices down. He then strode, with full steam ahead to his office. The teachers on bulletin board duty were not so quick to leave. Viola and I waited as the group slowly melted away, some to make phone calls home and spread the news, others to check the bulletin boards. Some like Candy and Dickie and Bill just might be meeting in the gym to discuss their future careers as teachers.

This was really evil, and it was lucky that we had time to fix it. Viola and I were suddenly in a silent hallway alone. He turned to me. "How are you feeling?"

"Better."

"Well, what do you think?"

I was thinking a lot of things, like could I buy Viola's cologne for Al? And what exactly was it?

I was thinking that maybe it wasn't Candy, Dickie and Bill who had posted the notice, unless that is, they were all working on a red herring. I was wondering why someone would be so angry that they would kill a student and destroy those cloaks. I still didn't know why someone wanted to blow me up. I finally answered Viola.

"I think it is not those three mentioned here who posted this but someone else. Dickie is not a good actor and he was really angry. Someone is trying to raise our suspicions so that we would follow these three around. I am not saying they're not up to something, possibly having to do with money and each other. I just don't see them as murderers. Maybe if they were driven to it, but I don't know that they would simple come together to do such a thing.

Bill is sneaky and likes fine things, he is the students' pal. I don't think he could kill a student. Dickie, killing someone, I could see if that person was out to make him work harder. But again, it would have to be a strong reason, which I don't see. But what if Booth had found something out about all three of them? Like the affair, or that Candy was giving them money from her grant? Maybe then they could kill. Candy, I think is out for Candy alone. She could have killed Booth if Booth threatened to expose her for the missing funds or the affair. Candy is very strong. She works out with weights in the dance classes she teaches. But we don't even know what Booth knew exactly. I am confused. What about you?"

Viola smiled at me. "I like your reasoning, I think I agree with some of it. But somehow there is a group of people involved in maybe drugs and money in this school. I also think that someone stole funds. Anyway, I am going to walk you to your room. Be careful tonight. I'll come by at the end of the evening to walk you to your car. Wait for me!"

"I will." Late night walk with Viola through the parking lot, who could ask for more?

We got to my room; of course, no one was there yet but me. Viola left me and I sat down at the ugly wooden teacher's desk and waited, grade book open, for the first parents to arrive. I never get many parents, so I knew I would have plenty of time to think about the murders. But I did not expect the arrival of some of my Nut Squad students. Mary, Jeff and Martha came in together. They were humming a tune. Jeff was softly playing his guitar as they entered. He took his guitar off and put it in a classroom closet.

"Hi Teach," said Jeff. Oh boy, could it get better than this? Where was a parent? I smiled at the students and said "Hi". The three of them threw themselves into chairs near my desk. Planning to stay.

Jeff spoke up. "We have something you have to see, Teach."

"Ok, what is it?"

"Nah, Teach, like we don't have it with us, like we found it and hid it." The two girls nodded. The nods were more than they had contributed to my class in months. I waited for further information.

Martha spoke up. "We hid it backstage. We'll show you."

"What exactly is it?" The three of them looked at each other. Somehow, they communicated something without words. I did not have a clue as to what they were thinking.

"No," piped up Mary, "we have to show you."

They looked at me. I sighed. If Viola found out I had left my room with anyone I think he would kill me. But I was not going to get any information from them by sitting here. I rose. I placed a note on my door dated and timed and stating that I would be back in 30 minutes. At least if Viola stopped by, he could start a search for me if I were not back. They rose and together we walked out the door, with Jeff leading the way to the auditorium.

I turned on all the house lights. There was no one in the auditorium. We all quietly walked up the stage steps and backstage past the destroyed green stage floor, into the wings. Martha took the lead. She brought us to one of the two backstage dressing rooms backstage. Backstage dressing rooms in a high school were a luxury. Most of the students used the cafeteria to dress in during the show. These dressing rooms were really for visiting actors who participated in shows at the school. I kept them locked.

Martha used a hairpin to unlock the door of the smaller dressing room. Well, I thought, I had to invest in new locks! There, sitting in the middle of the dressing room floor, was what looked like a gym bag. Martha whispered, "We found this in the closet where we store the lights and stuff for the stage. We were putting some lights away that we had back stage for the show. We got scared and wanted you to have it."

With those words I was getting scared too. Martha opened the bag. It was packed full of money! I could not believe that these students were turning it in to me. They were from poor homes, but they were honest! Then the thought hit me; who would hide all this cash here and why? Was it for a drug deal? "Children," I said calmly, so as not to panic them, "maybe we should take this back to my room and look for Detective Viola?" They all nodded again. When this group wasn't talking something was very wrong. "Did any of you see someone with this bag?"

"No Teach."

I turned to Jeff. "Jeff go and get me something to wrap this bag in. Look in the costume area for some long cloth."

Jeff ran to the garbage instead and grabbed the garbage bag. "Ok?"

"Great." All I wanted to do was get us all out of there, before the murderer missed the money. "Come on, let's go back to my room with this. Martha, close the door please."

Martha locked the door again with a hairpin (yes, I definitely needed new locks), and we moved swiftly through the auditorium. I was lugging a 30-pound garbage bag that felt full of money. We headed for my room. No parents were waiting to see me (not a surprise). I opened the door. We sat down together. I turned to Jeff. "Please go get Detective Viola for me. He is somewhere in the school. I need him to see this."

"I'm on it Teach!" He ran out the door. The girls stared at me.

"We will see what he says when he sees this. It was good of you girls to get me."

Martha spoke "Yeah, we think the money has something to do with Roberto's killing. And we all want his killer found. We know you do too, Teach. No one should get to use that money, if it has something to do with Roberto dying." I nodded, as I shoved the garbage bag under my desk for safekeeping. Together we waited for Viola.

"You're right, Martha." We continued to wait. Suddenly, I heard the intercom above my head crackle into life.

"Hey, ah, Detective V, guy, can you like walk to Ms. Teach's room? You know, Ms. Bruno, like needs you."

Jeff's loud voice sprang to life. Wonderful. Who in their right mind let Jeff into the Principal's office on Parents Night to use the intercom?

"Like come right away. It's like very important. Thanks D guy! Hey, principal dude, I was using that!" There was a cracking sound as if the microphone were being grabbed back and forth. Thus, ended the message. Well, now everyone in the school knew that I had information for Viola. Great! I might as well wear a target on my back to make things easier for the murderer.

A different voice came on the intercom. It was the Principal. "All teachers are to be in their rooms! Remember, parents have another hour to visit with you!" He sounded out of breath, as if he had just wrested the microphone from Jeff. Then we heard, "Give me back that microphone!"

"Ok, Princie Guy, Ok!" yelled Jeff.

The sound went dead on the intercom.

The two girls in my room laughed.

Viola hit my door.

111

"What happened?" He glanced at the two girls who were quietly doing their nails with a very smelly scarlet polish.

"Seems like Mary, Jeff and Martha have found something that we think you should have."

"What is it?"

I grabbed the garbage bag from under my desk, handed it to him. Then I walked over and locked my door.

"A garbage bag?" He frowned at me.

"Open it. There is another bag inside it."

He opened it. His eyes bugged. "Where did you find this?" he turned and asked the two girls.

Martha answered. "It was in the closet with the spare lights and stuff backstage. We thought it might have something to do with Roberto, so we told Teach. We want Roberto's killer to be arrested."

"We will make sure that happens. Thank you, girls for turning it in to me."

The two girls nodded. Mary said, "Well Teach see you soon. We have to go get Jeff and split. I guess he is with the new Princie." Both girls laughed, and waved their red nails at me. Mary took Jeff's guitar from the closet. She opened the locked door, and they walked out of the room.

"Did you count it?"

"No."

"Well, let's do it together. Can you put paper over the window in your door so no one can look in?"

"Sure." I did as he asked, and locked the door again. We counted and counted. There was $50,000 in the bag. All the bills looked used. We both counted again. The total was the same. We sat back in our chairs and looked at each other. I am sure we were both thinking where did the money come from and why?

Viola asked, "any ideas?"

"It is drug money or grant money," I guessed.

"Ok, but why leave it in the school, why not in a car trunk?"

"Maybe they're scared that their car will be searched," I commented.

"Is that what you think?" asked Viola.

"I don't know."

Viola looked at me and frowned. "Seems curious that this should show up where your students could find it after the police searched the backstage area twice. Did the students touch the bag?"

I nodded.

"We will have to get them fingerprinted to see if anyone else touched the bag. But the other things, such as the knife, sword and paint cans had no fingerprints. We are dealing with a crafty person here."

Fingerprinting my students. They will love that! I felt sorry for the poor police, they would ask them a million questions and try to get leads about the murders. Maybe the murderer thought that $50,000 would throw us off her/his trail? If the killer could give back this much money, how much money had been stolen?

"Maria!"

I jumped.

Viola smiled. "Can we go backstage now? You have 10 minutes of Parents Night left. Can you show me where they found this bag?"

A walk in the dark with Viola, what girl would turn that down? "Sure."

I turned off my lights, removed the paper from the window, locked the door and off we went.

At the auditorium door I turned on all the house lights again. We both looked around but saw no one in the auditorium. We crossed to the stage and entered the backstage area together. Then we saw it. Everything from the closets backstage, all the lights, cables, gels, cans of glue for the sets, and tools, had been thrown on the floor, as if someone had been searching for something. I groaned at the mess. It would take a week to clean all this up! The murderer must have been searching for the money. Luckily, the murderer had come back after the kids and I left the area.

Viola pushed me in back of him. He drew his gun. Immediately I broke out in a sweat. He had never pulled his gun before. Could there still be someone back here? He must have heard something. He held a finger up to his mouth, warning me to be silent.

I was frozen with panic. I couldn't have spoken if I wanted too.

We both listened and heard a crash from the dressing room area. Someone was throwing the furniture around. Now I was angry! Those dressing tables, makeup tables and chairs cost a lot from my budget. It had taken me five years of begging Booth to get that stuff. If the furniture was ruined, the newbie principal would not replace it so fast! Especially since Hamlet would not be running to make my theater budget any money this year! I started for the dressing rooms. Viola grabbed me and shoved me back, not letting me go. We had a silent mime argument while furniture bounced off the walls. The strange high whispering started as a piece was thrown with a crash!

"Oh, Maria," its voice whispered, the sound bouncing over the speakers through the sound system in the theater. This sick person was wired through my sound system and was using one of my expensive portable microphones! "Did you do this? Do you have my drug money? Maybe I need to pay you a visit at home tonight. Did you steal it from me?" My heart stopped. Al was home alone by now.

"Was it those bratty kids of yours that Nut Squad? Those kids have keys to everything. Maybe I will start with them. They are really nosy and stupid. They would love spending all that money."

I was frozen in position, listening. I knew that voice. Who was it? The whispering stopped. A door backstage right cracked open. Viola ran for the door, following the whisperer out. Something hit the doorframe with a crack, missing Viola's head by inches! The bell ending Parents Night rang. I stood, waiting for Viola.

A few minutes later Viola came back. He stopped by the door, took a handkerchief from his pocket and picked up the microphone from the doorway where the murderer had thrown it. That microphone was toast, it would never work again. I immediately thought about fingerprints. Maybe we would get lucky.

I peeled myself from the wall. "Did you see it?"

"No" he shook his head. "There was a whole group of teachers walking together to their cars from close to that door. Whoever it was could have just joined the group. Teachers were really walking swiftly to their cars. I never knew teachers could move so fast?" He looked upset.

Ha! What did you expect? No one wants to get grabbed by a late parent leaving the building or walking to his or her car after three hours of parent complaining.

Then I remembered what the whisperer had said. "We have to get someone to my apartment. Al is home alone. And you should see if someone can find Jeff, and my other students. This person is serious."

Voila put his gun away. He grabbed his phone and barked orders into it to protect the students and my apartment. I pulled out my cellphone and called Al, but there was no answer at the apartment. The tape picked up the message. I told him to be careful and that I was coming home. Viola grabbed my hand and we hurried to his unmarked police car.

"Someone will drive your car home. Let's go see if Al is Ok."

"I can drive."

"No!" he said. "No more bombs! We go in my car with my driver."

I hadn't even thought of another bomb. What a thought! I hurried to his car.

The driver, a young blond policeman, was already waiting for us. He seemed to know where to go as Viola jumped in the front seat after placing me in the back. "Buckle your seat belt," he ordered. I did. And thank goodness I did. We went home with siren blasting at about 90 miles an hour! The driver weaved in and out of the late-night Queens traffic. If my hair were not gray already under the blonde dye job, it would be gray after that ride home.

We pulled up in front of my building. Viola threw open the doors and we ran for the lobby. Tomas the night doorman was on duty. As Viola pushed a gold badge in his face and ran for the elevator buttons, I asked, "Has anyone come by my apartment tonight?"

"No Mrs. Cohen," he answered as he turned a page in the NY Post. Tomas had barely looked up to glance at Viola's gold badge. Viola was holding an elevator door open. I hurried to join him.

We got to my door. I used my key. There sat
Al, stockinged feet up on the sofa. When he saw
Viola in back of me he frowned.

Viola spoke first. "Hi, Al. Anything happen
here tonight?"

Al jumped up from the sofa. "Why? Was
something supposed to happen? Did you call
before? I was in the shower and heard the
phone."

Al looked at me.

"Yes, dear, I called. I am glad nothing
happened here. I had a boring night with no
parents." I passed the buck. Let Viola explain
this one to Al.

Al turned and looked at Viola. Al's eyes
narrowed. He realized he would not get a straight
answer from me.

Viola explained about the kids finding the cash,
and the broken-up furniture backstage and the
whisperer. Al was Ok until the whisperer. His
face went red. "What are you doing about this?"
Al asked.

Viola said that we would have a policeman
outside the building in case we got a late-night
visitor. Since our apartment was on the fourth
floor, there was no other way for anyone to get
into the building; the basement doors were locked
at night. With the police guarding our building
we should be perfectly safe.

We both said "Thank you." Al still did not look
happy. He opened the door and pointed to the
hallway.

"Good night, Detective."
Viola took the hint and left. Without another word, we went to bed.

19

"She Walks in Beauty Like the Night" (George G. Bryon)

The next day came quickly. I headed to work early and kept wondering about that voice. Was it really familiar? I was curious suddenly about someone both Viola and I had forgotten to interview, the beautiful Nan Summers, Dickie's secretary. She had appeared in my dream after Mrs. Booth was killed.

When I went to the lobby, the doorman told me that somehow the police had put my car back in its parking space in the basement.? How were they able to do that? I wondered. I must ask Viola.

I arrived at Dickie's office before eight thirty. Dickie, being the slug that he was, never really came to work before noon if he could help it. I knew Nan would be there alone. She was. Nan was tall, slender, and very beautiful. She had long hair that always shined. I really needed to ask her what she used on it! She wore simple pantsuits and flats to work. On the few occasions when she had joined us for school parties she wore stylish cocktail dresses, which always looked expensive. She looked surprised to see me.

I could imagine why. I guess in my 20 years of teaching I had only spoken to her maybe five times, and then it usually about a security issue. Did I mention she had a beautiful speaking voice too? It hardly seemed fair. She was beautiful and did not have one of those high squeaking voices she had a rich alto.

She was the brain behind the man, so to speak, if Dickie really had a brain. She did most of Dickie's work. I spoke first.

"Hi Nan, I have a few questions about what has been going on in the school lately and wondered if you could help me."

Her eyes narrowed.

"Is this about the money that your students found? If it is, Dickie is still with detective Viola about that. Viola called on Dickie at home this morning. He wanted to know if Dickie knew how the money got in the closet backstage. He asked Dickie over and over again. Dickie called me and told me what had happened before I left my house this morning. How would Dickie know anything?

Really, Maria, why are your students snooping around so much? There is a killer loose, and it could be dangerous for them." Did she really think I could control the Nut Squad? It is impossible. I would love to have her try it for a week!

Boy, handsome Viola was not letting any grass grow under his new Gucci shoes this morning. He must have gotten Dickie up out of bed. Dickie must have loved that!

She continued. "You know what a bad mood Dickie is in this morning? He hates coming in early. Can you believe that Detective Viola stopped by Dickie's house and got him out of bed to talk to him? And then, the principal, wanted the stage and auditorium locked up with new locks, which he and you alone is going to hold the keys to. He is very upset about your students running around finding things. Dickie is upset too."

I doubt the Principal was upset about my students. I thought he was very upset about a strange figure in black running around the stage trashing things.

She motioned me to one of Dickie's comfortable big chairs. I sat. The thought of Dickie getting dragged out in his nightclothes to face Viola was just too funny. I would have laughed, I think, if Nan had not looked so annoyed. The look on Nan's face made me curious. What exactly was the relationship between Nan and Dickie? Half of the faculty had a bet that they were having an affair. I sat and looked at her, wondering if she would give me any more news of what was going on.

She pasted a smile on her face and looked at me. "What questions do you have for me? I know you are working closely with Detective Viola. The principal told me I should help you both if I can."

"Do you know anything about who would be involved in what is happening here?"

She looked thoughtful. I waited.

"Are you asking me if Dickie was having an affair? I thought a lot of people knew that he was having an affair with Candy. It has been going on for years." She moved her chair closer to mine, as if she did not want the rusty basement pipes to hear what she was telling me. "I have known about it for years, and just thought everyone else did too. I really can't understand how Candy keeps both Dickie and Bill happy.

Maybe she keeps them on separate schedules, different nights? I never understood all three of them. It is really strange to me. I mean you look at Candy, she is very pretty, but kind of trashy, you know? I also think that she may be on drugs sometimes, because her eyes are red a lot when she comes down here to see Dickie during lunch hours. And I don't get it.

Why is she attracted to them? Bill is Ok, but he is really interested in younger women. Candy is now pushing into her late forties. I mean if I were Candy at her age, I would be looking for husband material. These two boys are not it. She is pretty enough to catch someone better. Bill still hangs in there, though. And Dickie, well, let's admit it Dickie is no catch, except his parents have money. He would have to divorce his wife. He is not smart, not ambitious, but very good looking.

According to what he has told me, his marriage is on the rocks. What is really going on among the three of them? I don't know. Do you?"

I shook my head no. I bit my tongue so I would not tell her that I knew for a fact she had five years on Candy. She had shown me her passport one day because it expired and she wanted to know what to do. I saw her birthdate. It seemed interesting that Dickie was sharing his marriage problems with his secretary.

"Do you think one of them could be dealing drugs to students? Could that be where the money came from?"

"Drugs! I hadn't thought of one of them as a dealer, but I don't think Dickie has the brains for it. He is just plain lazy."

I agreed with that view.

She went on. "If I was to guess I would say Candy is involved in something like that and maybe Bill. He is always down here with Dickie. And sometimes he comes with Candy. Bill is smarter than Dickie. Candy, grew up poor. That is what she shared with me one day when we went out for drinks after work, and if I had to bet on one of them being a survivor and able to plan a drug ring, it would be her. She never wants to be poor again. She told me so. Besides, under all that makeup, Candy is really slicker than the boys."

Bill, with his smart expensive clothes, his new car every other year, could he be a dealer? Where did he get the money from? Students were always hanging out in his room. Were they buying or selling? But how did Candy fit in? Was there really a drug ring as Nan thought? What about Booth and the money comments she had made? I got up.

"Thanks for the help, Nan."

She smiled. "Nice to see you, Maria. Hope to see you again."

As I walked away, I wondered why Nan was so very helpful. Was she jealous of Candy? Did she want to send me on a red herring away from her? Nan was surely smart enough to be a dealer herself. She ran rings around Dickie. Of course, anyone with half a brain could run rings around Dickie. Was she really trying to be helpful? Or to draw interest away from herself or Dickie? To quote, it was getting "curiouser and curiouser." (Lewis Carroll)

The students were off today for Prom Night, I just remembered. That was why I was not seeing any of them around, and why there were no announcements or bells this morning. Plus, I was a Prom chaperone, so I was not required to come to school today, since I would be at the Crow Restaurant with the students till midnight tonight. I made a mental note to go home and try to squeeze into my gown by eight o'clock for dinner and the dance. I had meant to lose ten pounds for Prom Night in order to get into my gown more easily. But as usual, it had slipped my mind. I really hated diets.

What a fun night to look forward to, checking for liquor in the punch, passed-out students in the bathroom, students hiding in dark corners doing goodness knows what. No wonder Al refused to go, even though the food was great. I wondered what faculty and staff would be there. I also wondered if Viola would be there. I went in search of him now.

I found him and another officer backstage. I winced when I walked in; one of the dressing rooms was a total wreck. Not a bit of furniture was left. "Can I talk to you?"

"Sure." He smiled that Mr. Perfect Smile.

I walked out of the room to center stage. He followed. I explained everything Nan had said. I also told him that I was beginning to feel as if everyone was lying for someone else. He nodded but said nothing. He was not giving anything away that he knew.

I was beginning to feel like his Watson in Sherlock Holmes. Except Holmes occasionally told Watson something about what he thought. Enough of this; I had a prom to attend! I told him I had to go home and dress and get my hair done for the prom that night.

He smiled at me again. "Save me a dance. I always liked dancing with you."

Oh boy! He would be there. He had been a great dancer. This could be interesting! I nodded. We were both practicing our nods, and I left for my car.

"Sergeant! Check Ms. Bruno's car, please," he yelled and a sergeant came running.

The sergeant checked my car front, back and underneath, and said I could go. He headed back inside. I was glad there was nothing. I did not know if our insurance would cover another bomb, or another new car!

I drove home. Al was glad I was home so fast and still in one piece. I reminded him about the prom and he was not so glad. I then told him Viola would be there and he frowned but said, "Good."

I told him I was going to the hairdressers after lunch. We had a pleasant lunch together and I left. At least Al's lunch looked yummy, mine looked like low-calorie grass. I went to the hairdressers and came back, shoved myself into a blue gown size 18, which must have been shrunk by the cleaners since last year, and dragged myself to the prom.

20

Rock and Roll, It's Prom Night!

Dickie was greeting students at the door. Two police officers stood with him. Some of the seniors looked at Dickie with confusion on their faces. As I walked past I heard one whisper to the other, "Who is he?" How could they know an Assistant Principal of Security who lived in the basement? They may have never even seen him when there was a fight! That's what teachers are for, according to Dickie.

All the students who knew me came by to say hello as I sat at a table in the dining room. I really like seniors, and them stopping by to talk to me made me feel great. I asked who was going to what schools in September. Even some of the Nut Squad from a few years ago, had gotten into community colleges, which made me very proud of them. All the girls looked lovely in their gowns, orange and yellow being "in" colors this year. All the boys in their rented tuxedos looked great too, and so handsome. It was hard to believe that four years had gone by so quickly. These children had entered my classes at 14. They'd been so awkward, tall and thin, and now, four years later they looked like well-groomed young adults. It really made a teacher think that she had done her job.

I walked past the banquet tables loaded with food. The food looked great. I had just returned, with a full plate, when I felt someone's arm around my waist. I yelped, turned quickly and the food went flying. Viola, whose arm it was, was fast on his feet, or he would have gotten a face full of pasta with meatballs.

"What are you doing?" I asked. I pasted a smile on my face. A waitress grabbed a mop and a broom. Viola, his arm back around my shoulders this time, led me to a seat at the principal's table. Not where I wanted to be! I whispered, "I don't want to sit here, and I want my food back!"

"I'm sorry about your food Maria. I'll get you another plate. I am so glad you decided to join me at the principal's table." He announced all this is a loud voice. I was steamed. Why would I want to join the principal? Why would I want to sit with Viola who was manipulating me?

He jogged off. I could only hope he was coming back with food! The principal's table was in a smaller room off the dance floor, separated from the students' dining and dancing area. This was so that the faculty members could talk to each other without going deaf from the blasting rock and roll music.

I was tempted to move, but I thought Viola would kill me. Tommie Newbie smiled at me. I smiled at him. We really had nothing to say to each other. I did not want to discuss the damage to the stage, that was for sure. The table looked like it was filled with a group of suspects from school. So that's why Viola wanted to sit here. This could be interesting.

Candy was at the table next to Bob. On the other side of Candy was the principal, who was staring at Candy's low-cut gown. Next to the principal was Nan Summers in a beautiful blue cocktail dress. Next to Nan was Bill, and next to Bill was Sheila, who was wearing a black gown with a turtleneck and long sleeves. Not a great look. Someone should tell Sheila how to dress for formal occasions. Of course, I should not judge poor Sheila as I sat here in a tight gown when I should be six sizes smaller. But she really needed a beauty consultant.

I felt like breaking into a chorus of "hail, hail, The gang's all here." There was an empty seat next to Sheila, and then Dickie took it. He stared at me, wondering perhaps what I was doing at the principal's table. What *was* I doing here? I stared back.

How could the principal have Dickie at his table when Dickie never did any work? Then here came the Handsome Detective, my ex-heartthrob, and he was carrying two plates heaped with food. I hadn't noticed how good he looked in some designer tux. Since I hadn't noticed till now, maybe I really needed food. I began to get into a better mood. He sat down next to me. He handed me a plate. What a prince! He spoke.

"So, this is very nice. The food looks great! Who is in charge of the prom?"

Bob spoke, "it rotates every year. But this year, it was Candy and Dickie's turn. They get a committee of students together that pick out the food they want to serve, and a band. The superintendent must approve the band. They also fundraise for the prom. They sell candy, do car washes, and sell tee shirts, things like that. And the two advisors have to attend all these affairs and make sure the students stay within a budget. They also are there to make sure the students are safe. It requires a lot of extra time from the teachers, for which they get paid very little."

Viola nodded.

Yeah, that's right. And that's why when my name came up for prom advisor in a few years I planned to be retired.

Bob continued. Tommie Newbie was nodding along with Bob's details and stuffing his face with food. How could a young guy eat so much so fast and stay so thin? Was he a jogger? Maybe he could join the Candy, Dickie, and Bill's jogging club?

"It is a lot of work and takes a lot of time. So, the teachers who do it should be congratulated. Congrats to Candy and Dickie!"

"Here! Here!" said the newbie.

"Here! Here!" echoed everyone else mildly.

Meanwhile they were all thinking, am I doing this next year? How can I get out of it? I stared at Viola. He was glancing around the table. I decided to eat, more daintily then Tommie.

I looked at the plate of food that Viola had brought me. It contained some of my favorite foods. I glanced at his plate. It was the same as mine but bigger portions. Oh No! We used to like the same foods, it seems we still did! This togetherness thing had got to stop! Al would kill me.

The room filled with conversation as the band set up for the dance and students went back to the buffet for thirds and to talk with their dates. Viola glanced at the band. If he was going to ask any questions, it had better be before the band started. It would be impossible to hear anything after that. Suddenly I decided to ask a few questions of my own.

"Does anyone know what happened with the grant funding that Booth had? Does it continue to be given to the school even after her death?" I asked innocently.

Bob gasped. Candy and Dickie and Bill looked at each other. They had strange expressions on their faces. Viola turned to me with a smile on his face. Tommie stopped eating and there was a pause. Sheila smiled at Tommie. I guess no one could believe that I would be so tasteless as to ask such a question.

Tommie spoke. "It depends on the grant, most grants run till they end, no matter who is in charge of the school. The dance grant was received in a lump form, so that money should be in the school accounts and be used for dance. Isn't that correct Candy?"

Candy pasted a smile on her face. "I guess so, but as I told you, Maria," she turned to me, "Booth was in charge of the funds. She gave me the funds as I asked for them."

Tommie frowned. "Hum, strange, because I thought in the accounts the funds were given to you directly for your programs." Tommie chewed on an egg roll thoughtfully. "I can check that, of course. Sheila, do you know?"

Sheila looked at Tommie with a frozen, almost drugged expression on her face. "What?" she asked.

Tommie sighed, stopped chewing and asked again as if she were an idiot, "Was the grant given to the dance department in a lump sum, or not?"

Sheila almost looked like a deer caught in headlights. Sheila turned to Bob. Bob answered. "Yeah, the grant was given to the department, but Booth gave out the funds in pieces. No one was ever allowed to have a ton of funds at once. Booth controlled the money, not the teachers."

Tommie frowned. He turned to Viola. "I will check it for you. The money should have gone to the dance department in one lump. Something about the distribution does not seem right."

I did not look at Tommie, because Candy, Dickie, Bob, Bill and Sheila looked like they had been hit by lightning. I mentally congratulated myself on asking the right question. Someone had more funding for something than they were supposed to have. Money, money, who has the money and what happened to it?

You have to follow the money. I had read many good mysteries and knew the drill. Viola acted like he wanted to ask something, but at that moment, the band started playing at its typical deafening level. Dickie grabbed Candy and literally dragged her to the dance floor. Bob stood and followed with Sheila. All four on the dance floor were talking animatedly as if they were having an argument. Bill stood and took Nan to dance.

Tommie stood and looking at Viola and me, screamed to be heard over the band, "I am going to walk around and check the corners out for students doing strange things. You really can't trust students in dark corners." I did not volunteer to join him.

Viola looked at me. I looked at him. We continued eating. Viola placed his head next to my ear. "Listen, partner, next time, let me know the plan before you ask the questions. I don't want you to get hurt. Someone already thinks you are too close to some answers."

I nodded. He was right. The band blasted on. He continued to speak into my ear. "So now we know a few people may have used the funds for themselves. Candy, Dickie, Bill, Bob and Sheila all looked guilty. Do you think they all are?"

It was impossible to speak over the noise without whispering in his ear. I wanted to skip that, so I shrugged. I finally gave in and dragged his head of full thick hair close to my mouth. "I don't know who did what, but I think they all did something. Maybe we can get one of them to crack. But the problem is, I can't see any of them as a murderer. A thief yes, a murderer no. For a group of teachers this is a lot of money. But I also wonder about the something else, like drugs. See, we have maybe drugs, murders, and grants involved. But are the teachers all involved in everything or only in something? That's the question."

Viola took back his head. The band suddenly finished their set. We had lost sight of the dancing teachers. My ears were ringing. As I've gotten older, I'm finding that it's taking longer for my hearing to come back after prom night. "We have to find the answer, if just to keep you and the Nut Squad safe," said Viola. I shivered. He was right. Then we heard it, a high-pitched woman's scream. It tore through the room over the heads of the students on the dance floor. We both stood up quickly. I counted teachers on the dance floor, but it was hard to see, as people started moving toward the screams.

Viola took my hand. "Police!" he shouted as we pushed our way toward the screams. The students, who had been taught to give way before authority, broke apart and gave us a path through the room. By the bathroom doors, Sheila stood like a statue, rigid, still screaming. Cops came through the crowd. One female cop took her by the arms and shook her. It made her stop. Sheila then pointed at her feet. We glanced down at her feet. Tommie, the newbie principal, lay there in a pool of blood. Someone had cracked his head open. Sheila's hands held a tire iron.

It was full of blood. Viola kneeled down to check Tommie for a pulse. The cops started to push the students back from the scene. One cop called for an ambulance. Viola said Tommie was still breathing. I took my wool shawl from my shoulders and draped it over Tommie to keep him warm. Viola nodded at me. One of the cops bagged the weapon in Sheila's hands and she was led out of the room.

The ambulance came. Viola sent a cop with Tommie, in case he woke up and talked. I was shocked. If I had not been so lazy, maybe I could have walked around with Tommie and this would not have happened to him. If I had not decided to treat the table discussion as a game, perhaps this would not have happened to him. Someone went after him while he walked around alone looking for students in corners. If he had not been alone it may have never happened. If I had not asked so many questions maybe this would have not happened. Cops filled the space near the bathrooms. They took all the faculty and students onto the dance floor and set up chairs so no one could leave before being questioned. It was going to be a long night.

Marge, Bob and Candy took the job of calling all the parents to come pick their kids as soon as possible. No one believed that a student in prom dress had done this to Tommie. They would be covered in blood. In fact, no one was covered in blood, which seemed strange to me. Sheila had blood on her hands but not on her clothes. If she had hit Tommie she would have had blood on her clothes. I thought she just picked up the weapon when she found him on the ground. Why had she done that? Had she seen anyone?

Several police officers arrived and started taking students in groups into another room and asking them questions. "Did anyone leave your group? Did you notice anything strange right before the screams? Was there anyone you noticed who did not belong to the school? Were you in the hallway when this happened?"

The kids stopped by and told me what they had been asked. I was seated in a folding chair in a blue funk. Nothing made sense. Unless someone thought Tommie, was getting close to discovering something?

Viola marched out of the student   interviews. He pulled over a chair and sat with me. I had nothing to say. I was feeling that Tommie getting hurt was my fault. He sat silent for a few minutes. I knew he would speak first. When I was engaged to Viola, the one thing I had discovered is that he did not like silences.

"I will get the books looked at again tomorrow. We should be able to figure out something from them, if Tommie thought he saw something. If we have to we can call in a police accountant."

I didn't place any bets on that. I too had a principal's certificate. And had taken a year-long class in boring school budgets. I still was not good at understanding budgets. If there was fudging, Booth had 30 years on me. She would have been able to really hide funds. I didn't know if Tommie was just lucky or he was very skilled at budgets. I didn't think he would lie. We needed Tommie awake and alive before we could find out anything.

At that moment, through the front doors marched the Superintendent, Dr. Kane, and his group of flunkies. They always followed him around. In all my years of teaching, no superintendent had walked into a school function without a group of suits following him. We had met once at a meeting. He made eye contact with me and marched toward me!

"Ms. Bruno," he spoke in a hard, loud voice, "what exactly happened here?"

I started to trip through an explanation. But Viola jumped in. He stood. "Perhaps we can go over into this corner and talk."

They walked off together. Eventually, the Superintendent called me over. I got up and approached him.

"I have spoken to Detective Viola and made a decision. Since you are in the school currently and know everyone involved, I want this case solved soon." He paused and I nodded. Over the years, I had found the less you comment to your boss, the safer you will be. He continued, "So I am making you acting principal until Tommie returns. You have a current Principal license. You are also the next ranking teacher in the building for a promotion from the principal pool. Since you would be a principal somewhere as soon as the next opening, you might as well be the acting principal at your own school."

My mouth dropped open. I had gotten a letter from the Department of Education saying that I was going to be placed in a school as an acting principal from the Principal Pool. I didn't think it would be so soon. I thought I might be retired before there was another opening. I tried to speak but couldn't. He just nodded at me. Since I did not speak, I guess he took my silence as agreement.

"The paperwork will be on your desk in the morning. Sign it and get to the bottom of this. And send these students home now!" He and his flunkies walked out as swiftly as they had arrived. Viola, the traitor, walked him to the door. I just stood there; I was frozen in place and could not move.

The thought of running a huge school with 4,000 students in it made me feel ill. I had wanted to be principal in a small, chic, arts high school. And this school, with all of the murders, made me even feel sicker. Viola walked back to my frozen body. I looked at him.

"I could kill you!"

"It was his idea."

"I never wanted to be a principal and never under these conditions," I whispered a little louder.

"Look upon it as helping the police and good job training," he whispered back a little louder. "Up till now, I really wanted you out of this investigation. But, that was before Tommie was hurt and I needed another Principal at Hassle

High. With you appointed Principal, I will have someone who can work with me to solve these cases. Think of it a penance for Tommie being hurt tonight after your questions."

"Are you out of your mind!" The heck with whispering.

The dance floor was still half full of students and some parents. They stopped talking and looked at me. I realized that Viola and I were having our second fight in 30 years. Not only that, but half of the senior class was watching it. I felt my face go beet red. "I will see you in my new *Principal's* office tomorrow morning, when I come in," I announced to Viola and the rest of the room.

He just smiled at me. He had always been a betrayer, I knew that from when he deserted me a week before our wedding, and now this! I turned and, slamming my high heels into the floor, all one inch of them, I walked myself out to my car. A good-looking young cop was by my car door. "I have orders to drive you home."

"Just great," sarcastically, "Who gave that order?"

"Detective Viola."

I gave up and surrendered to the police; my keys to the car, that is. The young good-looking cop dropped me at my apartment door. He knocked.

Al answered. "Viola called me." He opened the door. "I can't believe they made you principal!" He said after I thanked the young cop and sent him back to Viola. He smiled strangely. "Here is a job you always secretly wanted and now you got it. Maria, I think that in this situation you should retire. I am really concerned for your safety." He looked at me. "But, I know you won't until they find out who committed these murders. I expect, as I told Viola, he is to keep you alive." He kissed me. "We are going to bed now." And so, we did.

21

The School Is All Mine Now

The next morning, I can't begin to tell you, what a pleasure it was to get up later than usual, put on a good expensive suit and go to work in my new office. So, what if my secretary was in jail and one principal was dead and the other still unconscious? I had called the hospital first thing, in case Tommie was alive, well, and ready to take back his desk. He was not. So, I finally got to wear one of the expensive Channel suits in my closet that I had been secretly saving, as Al said, for the big day when I was made assistant principal or principal. I dressed in front of the mirror in a pink shell colored suit, staring at my blonde hair cut in a blunt style, and my hazel eyes. My olive skin didn't show many wrinkles yet, I always avoided the sun. I didn't look bad at my age, just plump. I needed to diet. Viola still looked great. I needed to slim down to keep up with him in this detecting business. I decided as I drove into work, that this was my school, my time, and I would help Viola solve these crimes before someone else, namely me, got hurt.

I marched into my office, and there at the secretary desk sat Nan Summers, Dickie's secretary. She stood, smiling sweetly. "Dickie and I thought you could use me until you find a new secretary."

I smiled back. This was excellent. Perhaps I could pump her for more information as she spent time with me. Maybe I could discover if she was really a dealer of drugs. Or was Dickie, Bill or Candy the leader of the drug ring? And what did drugs have to do with the grant and the murders? Was beautiful Nan involved in all of this, since she was smarter then Dickie or any of the others?

"What a nice thing for you and Dickie to do!" I answered, still smiling. She and I stood there looking at each other, deciding how to continue. She finally spoke.

"I made some coffee. Shall I bring it to your office? How do you like it?"

"Great! One milk no sugar. Thank you, Nan."

"No problem, I will get it now."

Why not? There was nothing else to do here yet. The superintendent had, due to Tommie being injured at the prom, canceled school for students today. I turned and walked into Booth's office. The office that was now mine. I looked at

Booth's ugly artwork and framed awards on the walls and decided that today I would have it all removed and replaced by students' art. I knew that one did not speak ill of the dead, but Principal Booth simply had no taste in artwork. Good, I thought, my first Principal decision! I had decided about the walls. I would put Nan in charge. Nan came in carrying my coffee. And in back of her was Viola, one hour early! I took a sip of coffee and waved Viola to a comfortable chair.

"I want all these walls bare by the end of the day," I told Nan.

She looked at me as if I were crazy.

"Then I want you to call the art department, have the art teachers pick the best student works for my office, and get them hung up as soon as possible."

She looked at me, again as if I were crazy." You're going to remove Booth's stuff?" She looked amazed. I smiled.

"Yes, and I want it done today. Box everything personal for Booth's family and put it in storage until they can pick it up."

She nodded. "I will call the custodians up." She walked out.

"Ah, exerting authority already?" he smiled.

"This is the only way people will start to take me seriously. Also, I think we should get a technician in from the police who can really find out what happened to that $100,000. It should be in Booth's books or on her computer."

"I want to send someone in today but it might interrupt your first day at the job." He smirked.

"Viola," I drew a big breath to stay calm, "It is really your fault I have this job in the first place. I don't really want it, and I want you to find out who is doing this stuff."

"No problem. You know that Smith is back? She refuses to take time off, but since she really can't work full time, I have assigned her to babysit you and to check the books and the computers. She has an accounting degree. She will be your shadow. Try not to get her killed this time, Ok?"

The only cop I was thinking of killing was the Italian one across from me. At least I really liked poor Smith.

"Great!"

"Seriously, I don't want you to do anything without Smith in this school. There is at least one killer, drugs, and a lot of strange things going on. I want you to check out on time every day at three with everyone else. No staying late in school no matter what work you have to do as principal. Smith can't work past that anyway, she is still under doctor's orders to work only half time. She will take you home.

I don't want teachers or staff in this building late alone. I am posting two male cops undercover with the students. I want to find out about the drugs. That may lead us to our murderer. The cops are Jake Henderson and Ray Jackson and they both look about seventeen.

They will join the after-school activities and try to make friends with the kids."

"Good idea. "He really had to be kidding about the principal leaving a building at three? No Principal left a building in New York City before five.

"I told Al you would be home by four and I told him about Smith." He frowned. "I know you Maria, just do it."

Just do it? He sounded like a sneaker commercial.

He got up, took his coffee, gulped it down. "I'll see you later. I am meeting my undercover cops now. Redesign the office today. Smith will be here after ten." He smiled at me and walked out.

I stared down at my empty desk. I really hated men who ordered women around, but maybe in this case, he was right. Let the faculty be shocked at the news that I was in charge. That news should shock someone. We'd see who stopped by today, and I could take notes. I also wanted to work on Nan and this would be a perfect day for it as we redesigned the office together.

There was a knock at the door. My first visitor! Nan came in and announced Smith.

I was so happy to see her. She looked pale, but not bad. I hugged her. She seemed surprised and thanked me for the flowers I had sent. I sat her down at the back of my office, where there was nothing on the walls and no one could bother her at work. I gave her Booth's desktop computer.

She asked if we could go through Booth's desk together looking for anything strange. I agreed and the search was on!

We started with the center top desk drawer. It was very neat. Paperclips, markers, a stapler and computer flash drives lay there in neat piles. Smith took the drives to see if anything was on them. There were the usual principal files, budget information, really bad students' files. The bad student files were interesting since I had thought Dickie would have those. But Booth was a control freak, so maybe that was why she had them. There were teacher files regarding observations that I would need to look through. By reading the files I would learn how Booth really felt about the teachers. I pushed the files aside. And then I saw it. A brown leather book at the very bottom of the drawer.

Smith and I reached for it together. She had a stronger grip. She placed it on my desk and opened it. It seemed to be in Booth's handwriting. We studied the first page together.

"It's written in code," Smith said.

"Seems to be."

We looked at each other, then started to flip through the other pages. Only 10 or so were written on. All written in the same code.

Smith stood. "I will take this to Viola."

"Wait a minute, let me make a copy." I walked to the end of the conference table and copied the pages with the code on them using Booth's copy machine, which was now mine.   I made two copies. One copy I went over and placed in my briefcase. The other copy I went to place in the safe in the office. I stopped myself before I opened it. "Who knew who had the combination to this safe?" Why lock it? I turned to Smith and handed her the extra copy. "Maybe you should hold onto this and we can figure it out."

"Good idea; we can work on it."

We smiled at each other. Smith tucked the book under her arm and walked to the door to find Viola. As she opened the door, Nan and the custodians arrived. Within 10 minutes all of Booth's awards, photos and terrible artwork had been removed from my office and boxed. I sat there staring at my empty highly polished wood desk.

It was much nicer than the one in my classroom! Actually, Booth's desk was nicer than any teacher's desk in the building. Mine had graffiti dug into it from past students. Boy! It was nice to have a beautiful polished desk, but I was beginning to worry that my days as principal might be numbered if the killer thought I was getting too close.

I really did not know exactly what I was getting close to. Facts, I thought, I need a list of facts! I opened the desk and took out a lined yellow pad and began to write down what I knew so far.

1. I found Booth, killed by a stab to the back with a letter opener. Her personal letter opener.

2. Everyone on staff knew I was meeting her that morning because she published all meetings in the weekly calendar. Whoever had killed her must have known I would find her body.
3. My Nut Squad said they knew Candy, Dickie and Bill were together a lot of time before and after school.
4. Roberto is killed during my play rehearsals. Did <u>Hamlet</u> the play have something to do with the murders? Or was the killer trying to tell me something?
5. Who stole from the grant? Did they steal the money to use it for drugs? Who was the school drug dealer?
6. Was it the only time they stole money? Did they steal just this one grant? Or was more money involved?
7. What did Booth mean when she said she would not be leaving alone? What did she have on someone else? What could she push them to do?
8. Why did someone try to blow me up? Does the killer think I know something and about what?
9. Who was the crazy person with me in the basement? Why did they not kill me after they tried to blow me up?
10. The affair among Candy, Dickie and Bill posted on the school bulletin board. Was this done only to embarrass them? Or was it done as a "red herring"?

11. The whisperer on stage and backstage. What exactly was that about? Was it using the stage to draw my attention?
12. The Nut Squad finds $50,000. Whose money was it? Was it drug money? Why leave it where kids could find it?
13. Tommie was nearly killed. Sheila was left holding the tire iron. Did she do it? Did she see the murderer?
14. I was made principal. Smith and I found a codebook. Booth wrote it. Why? Why did she write it in code? Was she afraid someone would read it and be angry? What was in the book?

I finished my list and sighed. I felt like it had helped me to put down everything. But I still didn't know the right answers.

Nan came into the room with two pieces of framed artwork from the students. The work was modern and brightly colored. It would brighten up the office. She hung the pieces for me. I decided the time for being subtle was past.

"Nan, do you think Sheila would hit Tommie?"

She frowned while hanging the pictures, straightened a frame, then replied. "No, I don't think Sheila could hurt anyone. She worked with Booth all those years and did not hit her over the head. And believe me, that is self-control!" She smiled and turned to look at me directly. "No, I can't see Sheila killing anyone. Can you?"

"I guess not." Vaguely.

"I have known Sheila a long time and been out with her double dating, and she is very religious and couldn't kill anyone. Sheila was a good secretary for Booth, because she was not very smart. She typed, did what she was told and did not ask questions. No, I think whatever is going on is being done by someone who is pretty smart. The strange whisperer thing, the drug money the kids found which was not well hidden, the killings, which were done without anyone getting caught so far, and Tommie. It almost seems to me Maria, as if two things are going on." She shook her head. "I'm glad I am not the police."

I smiled at her. "Thanks for hanging the drawings."

"You're welcome, I will be at my desk if you need anything." She walked out.

Smith came back. "Viola is on his way here."

I nodded and thanked her.

Nan had given me something to think about. Maybe we had a drug ring *and* a murderer? Suppose the two things were not connected. I sat at my desk and thought for a minute.

Viola came in with two very young-looking men. "Jake, Ray, meet Ms. Bruno."

We all shook hands. Yeah, these guys could be seniors easy. They looked like teenagers. In fact, they looked way too young to be cops.

Viola continued, "I wanted you to meet them, before they start tomorrow. They will try to fit into the 10th grade, as that seems be the one class that knows a lot. Plus, they could pass as 10th graders who failed like your Nut Squad."

"Absolutely, I think they should follow around my Nut Squad, they are the 10th graders who talk the most. They know a lot of somethings, and if they don't know something, they are good at finding it out. Here's their schedule. I'll inform their other teachers that they will be getting two new students."

I turned on the computer and sent an email to the teachers. As I was typing Viola walked the guys to the side door in my office to send them home. As the door opened, I told them "Class tomorrow is at 7:30. See you then."

I kept typing. Viola stood by the door. I finished typing. He was studying my paintings. He looked over at Smith working and spoke so both of us could hear him. "Maria, Smith, you both are to be careful the next couple of days. I think we are on the trail of some very bad people."

"I'll be careful."

"I'll watch out for Maria's back, chief."

Viola smiled at us both. "Finish up it's almost three o'clock and I want you both gone."

My first day as principal had flown by. And thank goodness no one was dead. Tomorrow was another story, with all the students back in the building. Who knew what would happen then? I walked to the front office, thanked Nan for her help, made a mental note to get a permanent secretary, and sent her home early. Thus, ended my first day as an administrator.

22

"Drugs, Drugs, Everywhere and Not a Drop to Drink."

My second day as principal arrived with all the upset students, the undercover cops, the real cops, psychologists, angry parents and everything else you could think of after a terrible prom and an injured principal. First thing I did was go down to Dickie's office and inform him that he would be without Nan for a few weeks until I hired someone to replace Sheila.

He seems very unconcerned when I walked in, with his feet up on the desk and his cellphone in hand. I notified him of the fact that Nan would be mine, and he almost waved me out of his office to continue his cellphone conversation on school time.

I did get him to hang up the phone when I informed him that I expected him to walk the halls every hour and if he did not, I would be putting a letter in his file! Poor Dickie actually was expected to do something! Nan who had been standing at her desk with the door open, got a huge smile on her face that Dickie couldn't see. A good time was had by all. Especially me!

I took Nan to the office, asked her to keep everyone who was not an emergency at bay, and to please bring me coffee. All parents I sent to the assistant principals, whom I had told would be fielding parents' questions today. I called the hospital to check on Tommie, who was still not awake, but stable. I was secretly hoping that he would return to his job as soon as possible and I could go back to full-time detecting with Viola and Smith. Smith was installed back in my office, same place as yesterday, after picking me up at home. I suspected that the only people who were happy with this arrangement were Viola and Al.

Smith was working on the codebook. I had spent a couple of hours with it last night. Al was very good at puzzles but he could not break it. He promised me that he would work on it during the day. We all hoped that if we stared at it long enough today, someone would find a clue. Nan came in with my coffee. In back of her was Viola, his usual good looking, well-dressed, intelligent self.

"How are Jake and Ray doing?" I asked.

They were in the Nut Squad's Math class with Megan. Why did they all have AP Math? Who did that schedule? Was it Booth's idea of a joke? Megan must be crazy by the end of first period.

He smiled and folded himself in a chair in front of my desk. "They're fine. I understand that they were both handfuls in high school, so they should fit right in."

"Great. I hope none of my teachers quit by the end of the day."

Viola laughed. That was a strange sound in the principal's office, I thought, someone laughing. "I had the cloaks, the letter opener, the knife/sword, and the jack from the car analyzed. Seems that our murderer does not do fingerprints. I am hopeful that Jake and Ray learn something quickly. We examined the grounds around the prom, and we found another Hamlet cloak with blood on it stuffed under a group of bushes. It was on the path leading to the parking lot. The lab says the blood was Tommie's but there are no fingerprints on it. No clues to our murderer."

At this point there was a hard knock on the side conference room door. Smith rose and went to answer it. I sank down in my desk chair; I wanted to hide under the desk if it was a parent.

It was Jake. He entered. Smith shut the door. The bell rang; first period was over. He walked quickly over to Viola and spoke.

"I was assigned a locker by the Assistant Principal of Security. I opened it for the first time just now. It is full of pot."

"Pot?" I asked.

"Pot," stated Viola.

"Pot," echoed Smith.

We all stared at Jake. There was a pause.

We all rose and I asked, "where is your locker?"

"On the second floor across from the boys' bathroom."

I took keys to lock my back-office door and grabbed a walkie-talkie from the top of my desk. I told Nan we would be back in ten minutes and we all went out the side door, which was closer to the boys' bathroom. Up the stairs we tripped, walking through very noisy crowded groups of students.

"Get to class, get to class!" I said loudly, as I have been saying for 20 years. No student seemed to move any faster than before I became principal. I waited at the top of the stairs for Viola, Jake and Smith. I turned to Jake. "Show me."

Jake took out his lock combination written on paper from his jean's pants pocket.

I had a thought. "Wait until the halls are clear of students."

"Otherwise we will have a crowd in 10 seconds," I whispered to Viola.

He told Jake to wait. I stood in the hall with the three cops. A few students said "Good morning, Ms. Bruno" as they walked by. I nodded, "Good morning".

We waited. The late bell rang. And then, from Megan's AP Math class came the Nut Squad, late as usual for their next class. They saw us standing there.

"Hi principal teach" said Jeff "like what's going on?"

I smiled at them all. "Nothing. We just thought we would see how the halls are clearing and write detention notices for students who are late to class."

"Oh, Ok, teach, or I mean principal, like we'll go to the Italian next, but you know we can't do foreign stuff. If you need us, come get us. You know we can help you solve the murders."

And with that they actually walked faster down the hall to class. It was a miracle! I turned to Viola, my mouth frozen from smiling. "Should I send for Dickie?" After all, Dickie was the Assistant Principal of Security.

Viola frowned. "I guess we could wait for him to get here. I would love to see his reaction."

So, would I.

I spoke into the walkie-talkie. "Mr. Somers, this is the principal. Report to me immediately at the boys' restroom on the second floor!" That should get him here.

"On my way, Chief!" Oh Boy, Dickie was calling me Chief!

Dickie took the stairs two at a time. Dickie was the laziest man I know. It was quite a sight to see that he could move rapidly. Go into his office anytime and he is sat with his feet up. He never moved quickly for fights or riots. This time that was not true.

Jake opened the locker. There, stacked in neat piles were the smallest little packets I had ever seen. The piles filled the locker to the top. Yes, there is a lot of pot there! Viola and I were both facing sideways to get a look at Dickie's face; it was as white as the boys' bathroom floor when it was clean. He seemed very surprised.

"Well", said Viola looking at him, "do you know anything about this? You are the head of security for this school."

"Me! Why me? I just have the empty lockers cleaned and give them to the new students. What about, ah, Jake here? Does he know anything? When I assigned that locker, it was empty. Maybe he has made some fast friends in the school?" Dickie looked at Jake with suspicion. Viola turned to Jake.

"We will talk to you in the office young man." I piped in. "Yes, Jake, go wait in my office." I did not want Dickie to know he was a cop. Viola turned back to Dickie as Jake without a word walked down the stairs heading for my office.

"You haven't noticed anything? Noticed any drug deals in school? No students being in this hallway when they were not meant to be?"

Dickie frowned his forehead wrinkling up in thought, "no."

"I want all the lockers in this section opened immediately," I stated.

"I have to get my keys."

I looked at him. He sighed. "I am going back to the office to get the master keys."
He walked off.

Viola called over his phone for one of the cops in the building to bring up evidence bags to take the pot and check for fingerprints.

"Maybe someone knows or suspects that Jake is a cop," I said.

Viola frowned. He was cute when he frowned. I had forgotten how cute he could be. "I don't think so. I think the killer is playing games, especially with the new principal."

Now I frowned. "Maybe."

Dickie ran back up the stairs with the master keys in his hand. Who knew he was so athletic? Usually in school when there was an emergency he moved like a slug. The uniformed cop arrived and began to empty the locker, using gloves. Dickie opened the lockers on each side of Jake. Then his eyes popped.

Both of them were full of pot.

This could be a long day. Now we had three lockers filled with pot. Dickie opened the others that were not assigned to students. They were empty, thank goodness!

"Ah Detective Viola," the uniformed cop spoke.

Viola was walking with Dickie back to me.

"There is a note here, sir."

Viola came back swiftly. I tried to peek over the cop's shoulder to see the note, but he was too tall. Viola asked for a glove and removed the note. He read it and turned to me. "Do not touch it."

Really, I was not dumb.

He held it and I read it aloud. "A gift for the new principal." Lucky me. Dickie looked at me strangely. He was still kind of white in the face.

I looked at Dickie strangely. Why was he so pale?

Viola looked at both of us strangely. What did Viola think was going on?

I turned to Dickie. "I want every locker in this building checked today. I don't care how long it takes you or if you have to stay late to do it. Detective, please assign a police person to Dickie in case he finds more drugs in lockers." My second order as principal to an assistant principal and it was a beaut! I glanced at Viola.

"Sure." He phoned downstairs for help for Dickie.

I looked at Dickie. He was upset, I could tell. He was looking at the floor. I wondered what plans of his I was wrecking. I stared at him. "Well?"

He glanced up from the floor. "I'll do it."

"Good." I did not trust him as far as I could have kicked him at that moment as I turned away and headed back for my office, I was sure Dickie knew something.

Jake, sat in a chair in Nan's outer office reading a Marvel comic book. Oh boy, I thought, what is today turning into? This guy really took undercover work seriously. He really wanted people to think he was a teenager.

"Young man, you come with me."

We headed into my office. Jake still carried the comic.

"Seems your locker was not the only one, young man," I closed my door.

I stopped the principal to student act. "We are waiting for Viola."

As if on cue Viola entered, ushered in by Nan. "We did not find anything else so far. But Dickie has miles of lockers to check yet." He smiled.

"He did not look happy about it either."

I smiled back at him. He turned to Jake. "Please continue your schedule for us, officer."

Jake stood, nodded at us both and left, taking the comic book with him.

Smith spoke up. "I think I have a handle on the code, sir."

I had forgotten she was there. Viola and I moved as one to her side of the office. She pointed to a line in which some names seemed to be written in code. "I figured out one; see here, this letter or symbol repeats over and over again, so I took that to be a vowel. I made it an *e*. Then I took the faculty list and placed that symbol as an *e*. Then from there I tried *a* and *I* letters I was able to figure out. *Mecca*. Once I had that, I started listing the funds that were next to his name. Seems like it is over $50,000."

Oh, Bill, what have you done?

"Good," said Viola. "Do we know what the money is for?"

Smith shook her head. "It could be drug sales?" hesitantly.

"Or it could be part of the grant from the dance department," He turned to me. "Why would Bill have part of the dance funds? Could there be a legal reason?"

"Yes, Booth could have moved money around to use for Mecca and his Italian classes. She was not supposed to do that, but who would stop her, unless there was an audit? She was an experienced principal. She knew how to move funds back and forth so that she could spend money as needed. But that is a pile of money, and Mecca should have a record of it if she gave it to him and he used it. The codebook seems like a fishy record to me. But with Booth, who knows? We would have to prove that Mecca used the funds for something else or as drug money. I can call him in and ask. But will he tell the truth? Or will he just say it was money for his courses? If he has receipts we would have to accept them. We would need more proof. Should I call him in anyway and see what he says?"

Viola thought for a minute. "Yes, I want to see his face when you tell him what we have found. We are not finding solutions to the murders, so let's start pushing people around a little. I sent the pot to the lab; maybe we will get lucky with prints. Smith, I want you out of the room when we talk to him. I don't want you involved with the code. I don't want anyone after you again. Go to lunch."

Without a word, Smith got up and walked out.

23

Confession is Good for The Soul.

I noticed I was not included in the out to lunch group. So, it seemed that no one was worried about my life at this point. One of the joys of being an administrator. You are replaceable. I headed to the phone. Before I could call Mecca's room the phone rang. I answered it and handed it to Viola. "It's for you."

Viola listened for a minute. He glanced at me, said "Thanks" and hung up. He turned to me. "Want lunch at the hospital?"

I looked at him. "Why?"

"Seems Tommie woke up."

I grinned at him, "Sure. Thank goodness he is awake. Maybe he wants his desk back. I just redecorated the walls. I hope he will be happy here."

"Not so fast. You and I have to see Mecca this afternoon when we get back."

I grabbed my coat. Told Nan we were going to the hospital and that Tommie was awake. "Thank goodness!"

"Yeah," said Viola. "Let everyone who asks know. And keep a list for me of who asks." Nan nodded.

I thought about that as we headed for the door together. Was he really trying to upset the murderer? Maybe we could get someone into make a move. I went back in the office and took the codebook. I handed it to him. "This is safer in your police car." I said in a whisper as we headed for the front door. He took it and locked it in his trunk. We both got into his car and headed for the hospital. We walked up to Tommie's hospital door, and there sat a policeman, probably there to prevent Tommie from being killed as he lay in bed.

Viola and I entered the room together. Tommie had a bandaged head. He looked like hell. He smiled at us weakly. A very young, good-looking woman in a red suit was holding his hand. She introduced herself to Viola and me, "Hi, I am Georgia, Tommie's wife." Who knew Tommie Newbie had a wife? He looked 12 years old. Viola shook hands and then got right to his questions.

"Do you remember what happened to you and who hit you?"

Tommie made a face as if he were thinking of something difficult. "No. All I remember is someone came at me in the dark hall near the bathrooms with a metal object in their hands. I knew it was metal because it shined. The person was very tall, taller than me. I think it was a man. The next thing I remember is waking up a little bit, to Sheila screaming and she was holding a metal object. But she could not have hit me, because she was in back of me in the hall, and whoever hit me stepped out of one of the bathrooms in the dark. I saw a door open. Why were the bathrooms dark?"

Viola answered, "Someone had broken the lights in the hall and bathroom. Are you sure you don't remember anything about the person?"

Tommie turned paler if such a thing were possible. "No. Tommie looked at me. "Maria you have to follow the money in that grant if you want answers. That's what I mentioned at the prom and that's what I think led to me getting hit. The superintendent called me and said he put you in charge. You need to be very careful. Someone doesn't care who they kill." He sighed. Georgia spoke up.

"I think my husband needs to rest. Please let him. Also, we both appreciate the police protection. The doctors said he should be home in a few days. But it will be quite a while before he can return to work. You are welcome to visit him, once I get him home."

What did she mean "quite a while" until he can work? That meant I was stuck being principal. Oh joy!

Viola addressed her. "You will have police at home, too, until I can solve these murders. We may have more questions in a few days. Thank you." I smiled at them both, and we thanked Tommie and left.

We went down to the hospital cafeteria and ate old wilted lettuce salads for lunch. Viola spoke up. "Let's go back and interview Mecca together. I do not want you to say anything. Let me do the questioning. If he is involved, I don't want him to think you have any extra information."

Oh yeah, I know all about the little woman being quiet. Who did Viola think he is eating lunch with? Had he forgotten how independent I was? I must have made a face, because he continued with his monologue.

"I really do not want you injured Maria. This murderer has chased you around, tried to blow you up, and sent you pot for gifts. I want you alive at the end of this. Please let me do my job."

I sighed. "Ok, Ok, but don't forget it is my office and if Mecca did it, I really want some answers. Since we are speaking of questions and answers, maybe you can answer one for me?" Viola nodded.

I took a breath and popped the big question that had been bothering me for 30 years.

"Why didn't you want to get married? You never even explained what was going on to me," I asked. I was surprised I asked him. It was a very awkward question to ask him after all this time. I really had to know.

"I was dating Brenda before I dated you that year. Do you remember?" He didn't look happy.

"Yes," I answered. Who could not remember Brenda the Bombshell? She hated me. I waited for him to continue.

"A week before we were going to get married, she told me she was pregnant. She claimed the baby was mine. I had to marry her. That was what you did back then. A week after you and I were supposed to be married, I married Brenda. 3 months later, I found out she was not pregnant. She lied to me to get married. She didn't want me to marry you. She was always envious of you. I didn't want you to know I made a mistake. I really could not explain it to you. I divorced her after a year. But you had already married Al. It was too late for us."

I stared at him. I could kill him for not explaining it to me many years ago. We could have fixed this together. I thought it was something I had done to him. "I thought I had done something," I said weakly. "I wish you had told me."

"Maria, I couldn't. I am sorry. It is the past. Let's go on with the present. My feelings for you now are almost as strong as my feelings for you then. But you are married to Al, and I don't want to interfere with your marriage. It really takes a lot for me to tell you this. But perhaps with time you can feel something more than friendship for me too?"

Why did I feel like I still wanted to throw my salad at him? I was totally confused by this confession from Joe. I was married to Al. Al had feelings too. But I was getting fonder of Joe every day we worked on these murders together. What were my feelings? "Joe, I am fond of you, but I really have to think about this. Are we just attracted to each other because we are seeing each other again? A great deal of time has gone by since we were together. My life has changed.

Al is my husband and he loves me. I won't hurt him for the world. I need time."

Viola got up and I got up. There was a silence. "Maria, I can give you time. Let's go back to school now. I hope we get some answers from Mecca."

What could I say? We headed back to the school.

24

Truth, What Is Truth?

In the car heading back to the school, I used my cellphone to call Nan and ask her to get Bill Mecca to wait in my office for me. As we walked into my office, Nan was in her coat standing by her computer. She nodded to my office door. "He's in there. Smith is with him. I am going home."

"Have a good night," I said.

She smiled and left. Viola and I headed for my office. He held the door and I waltzed in. Bill sat in one of the chairs in front of my desk. I sat in back of my desk. Smith got up and left the room as per Viola's instructions. For sure he did not want Smith hurt. Viola sat next to Bill. I said nothing, waiting for Viola to take the lead in the interview.

"Mr. Mecca, it has come to our attention in a record left by Ms. Booth that you received

$50,000 from her. Could you explain that to us, please?"

Bill frowned at him. "Sure; she got a grant and I needed new books and supplies for my courses. She advanced me the money in lieu of my application for a grant from the government, which has not been given out yet. I filed for a $100,000 federal grant for foreign languages in low-performing high schools. It was granted six months ago, but the funds still had not arrived, according to Booth. So, she advanced me some funds. That's why I am listed for $50,000. Of course, I don't know where that $50,000 she advanced me really came from." He stopped and smiled at us. "Any other questions?"

"Yeah. It seems like a lot for book funds. Do you have the receipts?"

"Sure, but I gave a lot of the receipts to Booth three months ago. I have copies, though. Would you like them? About $20,000 is still in the student government accounts for my use for senior projects and trips. You can check with Dickie. I think he is in charge of the student government fund; right, Maria?"

Since I had been ordered not to speak. I nodded.

"Seems," Viola continued after a strange look at me, "that today we found a large amount of pot in the school. Do you have any idea as to how it got here?"

"Pot?" said Bill.

"Pot," said Viola.

"Pot," I said. The only word I spoke and still Viola gave me a dark glance. I nodded again at Bill, who had glanced at me. He had to be wondering why I was not speaking.

"Oh no! I don't know anything about drugs. No senior girl has mentioned anything to me. I don't stand for any drug talk in my room. If you like, I will keep my ears open, though. If there is nothing else, I would like to go. I have a hot date tonight, and I've got to get changed. This girl doesn't like to be kept waiting." He stood up.

Why did Bill sometimes make my skin crawl? I hoped the girl was of legal age.

Viola stood too, "Smith!" Smith came back from Nan's office. "Walk Mr. Mecca out of the building to his car, please." Smith walked out the door with Mecca. He turned.

"Good night, and you might want to check with Dickie," said Bill.

"Oh, we plan to," answered Viola.

Bill left.

Viola looked at me. I still said nothing. "Well?"

"Oh," I said, smiling sweetly. "Can I talk now?"

Viola frowned at me.

I spoke. "Are you going to wait for Dickie to complete the locker check? Perhaps if you join him now, wherever he is in the building you can question him regarding the huge amount of money Bill received for books. I don't believe it! Where is the rest of that money? Also, I would like to find out exactly what funds are in the student government accounts. Seems like a lot to me!" I marched over to the building microphone. I was still steamed about not being able to question Bill.

"Mr. Somers," I barked over the PA system, "call me immediately with your location!" Ten seconds later my phone rang. It was Dickie. He said he was on the third floor. I told him Viola would be up to join him. He sounded nervous to me, but I had had it. I wanted to go home. Smith walked back in. "Smith, I want to go home now." Smith nodded. She said good night to Viola, I just nodded, and we trooped out to her unmarked car for my ride home. What a day!

The next morning dawned cloudy, like my thoughts. I wanted to know one fact today either about the money, the murders or the drugs. I decided in bed last night that Viola had told me what I needed to know about us. I could move on now. I needed to decide of what exactly I wanted from life. Did I want my marriage to continue, or did I want an exciting change with Viola? And I would have to think about why; why did I want a change? What about Al? I didn't really know what I wanted at this point. I would think about my future once Joe and I solved these crimes.

Smith had stayed over and we three Al, Smith and I, had worked on the codebook and gotten one more name out of it. Al was the one who found the answer, he was really good at puzzles. Guess who? Dickie was the lucky winner.

Seems Booth had given him $75,000 for the student fund. What the heck did Dickie have to do with student funds? He was Assistant Principal of Security. That money could have bought a lot of school security cameras. It had not purchased anything, according to the budget. So where was that money? Dickie had the drugs and the money to answer for today. But first we would tell Viola.

Suddenly I had an idea. Who in the building was really good at funds and accounting? The math department. Maybe one of them was involved in this? Smith and I got to school and Nan was sitting at her desk. "Coffee is ready and on your desk."

"Thank you." Boy, was she organized! I could get used to her being all mine.

"And Detective Viola is in your office."

Great. I walked in. Viola was leaning back in a chair, coffee in hand. He was sitting with his Gucci shoes on my desk, making himself right at home. I sat, picked up my cup and had a sip of coffee. It was hot. How did Nan know exactly when to pour it? I liked her more and more.

Viola spoke first. "Seems there are no more lockers full of drugs, which is a good thing. The undercover cops are in their classes. I told them to try to make a drug buy and see what happens. But our drug dealer may be lying low now that we've found their stuff."

Smith jumped in and explained about Dickie and the funds. Viola shook his head. "Some staff we have here. Guess we have to have Dickie come up now. By the way," he pointed to a pile of papers on my desk, "seems Mecca did have the receipts. Smith, you'll have to check them out."

Smith nodded, took the papers off my desk and headed back into the corner, where she had a computer set-up.

"You want Dickie now," I asked.

"Yep, no time like the present."

I called his office. No one picked up. Dickie was probably hiding I thought. I walkie-talkied him. He answered. "Yes Chief."

"Come to my office."

"Be right there."

Dickie came in, ushered by Nan. I thanked her. "Dickie," I said, before Viola could jump in, "do you know how much money is in the student fund?"

Dickie frowned. "I think about $100,000 or so. I told Viola that last night." Of course, Viola had not called and told me. Viola nodded. I frowned at him; a little shared information would go a long way in this case.

"Why so much money?"

"Gee, Maria, that you would have to ask Booth. I don't know. She gave me deposits and I sent them to the bank, where they were entered them into the account."

I turned to Smith, "Smith, can you check to see if the money is in that account and if so, who has access to it?"

"Yes."

I smiled at Dickie. "Seems we found your name in a book Booth left with $75,000 written next to your name." I paused and waited for a reply. Dickie's face had turned a little bit whiter. I waited. Viola just looked at Dickie and me.

Dickie finally spoke up. "I don't know anything about any money, especially that much money." We all sat for a minute in silence.

Dickie got up. "Anything else? If not, I will be in my office."

Viola, Smith, and I said nothing. Dickie walked out. Now what?

Viola turned to Smith. "See what you can find out." We both sat, drank coffee and thought. I started returning some phone calls from the pile on my desk, mostly parents with questions about security issues. I gave them Dickie's phone number. Viola smiled as I referred one after another of the parents to Dickie. We were both thinking the same thing. Let him work for a change.

Smith stood over my desk and next to Viola's chair. "There are a few names listed on the account designating people who could withdraw funds. They are Megan, Candy, Dickie, Bill and Bob."

"Great!" I replied. "I can understand Candy, Dickie and Bill. They would need access for prom, senior trip, etc. Bob is the assistant principal for Candy and Bill, so he is responsible for their bills, but why Megan? Is it because she is a math teacher and did the books? I am beginning to wish Booth had been a little clearer in her notes."

"What is the balance?" asked Viola.

"Currently there is $5,000 left. Before Booth was killed there was a balance of $320,000." answered Smith.

"What!" I said. "Where did all that money go?" Smith shrugged.

"Who signed for it?" Viola asked.

Smith replied. "We have Bill's and Dickie's stories, but a pile of money was signed out by Megan. According to the bank, she is the treasurer. Candy took $10,000. Megan took $100,000 right after Booth died."

My mouth hung open. "How much? She took how much?" Smith looked at me. I could not believe it. Megan was a nice person. Not a good teacher, true. But she was related to the mayor. There was plenty of inherited money in her background. What was she doing with that money? Why would she take it? It did not make sense.

Viola appeared to share my look. Smith looked at us both. Viola turned to Smith. "This maybe a legal issue but go get her and bring her to the office."

"She should be in her classroom teaching; it's room 235." I took a phone and called the class next door to Megan's room. The teacher agreed to combine her class and Megan's in one room. I said we had an emergency.

Smith went quickly out the door. He turned to me. "Expect her to say nothing when she comes in, but to ask for a lawyer. Her father has a big reputation to protect. He works with the mayor. They are related."

I could do nothing but nod. I couldn't believe it of sweet, not too bright Megan. Megan the Murderer did not ring true.

"Viola, did someone set her up?" I asked. He turned to me.

"I don't know. Let's see." His phone rang. "Ok," he answered and hung up.

"Sheila made bail." He looked at me. "The superintendent called and said he was putting her on a leave until the trial. She is not to come near the school. He personally explained that to her. Her mother has had her visited by a shrink. The shrink is sending her to a psychiatric hospital for observation. Seems when the doctor talked to her, her hatred and confused relationship with Booth really came out. Booth was always belittling her. The doctor told the superintendent that Sheila seemed really glad that Booth was dead. But, he doesn't think she could have killed anyone."

"Thank goodness!"

He glanced again at his phone, "The lab just texted me. From the angle at which the principal was hit, it had to be by someone at least six feet tall. Sheila couldn't have done it, she isn't tall enough. Why she picked up the tire iron, I don't know." He glanced at me. "You are out of the running too." He smiled. I laughed.

When I stopped laughing I thought, did he consider me a suspect? How strange! I stand barely five feet tall. I had been with him all night at the prom. I guess that helped rule me out. I suppose I should have felt flattered. But it got me thinking, who on staff was that tall? Most of the men were tall and so were a few of the woman teachers.

Smith entered with Megan. Megan smiled and sat in a chair facing me. She did not look guilty. Viola spoke up.

"Why did you sign out $100.000 from the school accounts after Booth was found dead?"

"Oh," answered Megan, "I was wondering when you would ask me about that. See, Booth asked me to move the money into her accounts at home. But I didn't get a chance to do it before she died. Would you like me to redeposit it back into the school account?" She addressed the last question to me. I looked at Viola. I could not believe what I was hearing.

I then asked Megan, "Did she ask you to do this often?"

She smiled at me, as if it were not a strange request. "In the last three years or so, maybe five times. I never really knew why. You know her, Maria, she did not explain things. I believed that she had a personal reason, but I did not ask her."

"Was the money always returned to the account?" asked Viola.

"Well, I don't know. Bob and the others might know. I didn't follow the balance that closely. I only did what she told me to do."

Viola looked puzzled. "You really never wondered?"

Megan laughed. "I grew up in a political household. There were many financial things that were strange. I learned growing up not to ask questions about money. Maybe that is why she came to me when she needed funds, and not the other faculty members, who might ask questions. I knew from experience that principals could basically move money around without question as long as things balanced out in the end. Isn't that right, Maria?"

All I could do was nod. She had a point. But what did Booth use that money for if only for a short amount of time? Investments? Stocks? Buying drugs? What?

Viola spoke. "Please return the money to the account in the next day or so and show us a receipt. We are trying to figure out the funds from Booth's accounts and the school budget."

Megan nodded and stood up. "I will do it after school today." She walked out.

I asked Viola, "What do you think she did with the funds, if only for a short time? Or did she keep some funds permanently?"

Smith spoke up. "I will check the last five years. But I also found that Booth made a bank withdrawal a month before her death. The amount was $200,000."

So that was why the account was so low. Viola laughed. He shook his head. "We will be looking for these funds for days. Smith, see if anything from that amount was deposited in Booth's account."

"Ok."

My phone rang. It was Nan. "Jake is here for you."

"Send him in."

Jake came in, still carrying the same comic book. He was blowing bubbles with a wad of gum in his month. He was picking up some bad habits from the Nut Squad. He saluted Viola once Nan closed the office door. "I was sent to remind you by the Nut Squad that the Senior and Sophomore Car Wash and picnic is about to start. They said to remind you that the principal cooks hot dogs. They also said that they eat a lot of them."

25

"Talking about the Car Wash" (Rose Royce)

Damn, I had forgotten I had to cook hot dogs, a
food I especially detest. What fun! I hoped the
cafeteria staff had remembered to order
everything for the picnic. I smiled at the very
young policeman. "Thanks Jake, I will be right
there."
Jake saluted again and left. Viola frowned at
the second salute. I said, "I think he is becoming
like the Nut Squad." Viola laughed. We stood
up.
"I hope you are good at turning hot dogs," I
said, "I hate them."
Viola and I headed for the courtyard between
the wings of the building where the grills were
set up. "How can an Italian hate hot dogs?" he
asked.
"I don't know. I have never liked them."
"Well, let's not forget to bring one back for
Smith. She loves them."
I felt the green-eyed monster start to grow in
my brain. How did he know that Smith loved hot
dogs? Did he and she have them on a stakeout?
What exactly was their relationship? I stopped
myself from opening my mouth and followed
him into the courtyard. I was beginning to get
quite fond of Viola. I had to keep reminding
myself that I was a married woman.

The kitchen staff was in the courtyard and all the picnic stuff looked great. I went to our head chef, Pierre, and thanked him for the set-up.

He said, "I know you don't like hot dogs so two of the kitchen staff have volunteered to cook for you. Besides, it's a lot of seniors and sophomores to cook for at one time. And this way you can sit and eat with them and also go see the car wash. It is hard to be a new principal the first week."

I thanked him and told him how nice it was that he had thought of me.

"Maria, you have been at this school a long, long time. We take care of each other." He smiled and turned back to unpacking supplies. Viola was at the first table eating a pickle. I waved him over and said, "I am going to the car wash out front to see how it is going. Do you want to come?"

He shoved the rest of the pickle in his mouth and nodded. I headed to the side door that exited to the front of the school where the car wash was being held. Candy, Dickie and Bill should be there, as they were in charge of the seniors and sophomores. Besides, it was a student fundraiser. I turned to Viola, who had swallowed his pickle, and said, "This was a big fund raiser for the school over the years. It has in the past paid for the senior trip."

"There is a senior trip?"

"Yes, I think it is the end of next week."

"We may have to cancel that if something else happens, Maria."

"We will have to see," was my answer. I disliked denying the students, unless it was necessary. I was watching the Nut Squad wash cars. They seemed to be enjoying getting very wet. Candy was standing there trying to supervise, in very short shorts, which of course she could wear, and what looked like a wet t-shirt. The t-shirt did not look like it was part of the faculty dress code. But I did not plan to have that discussion my first week. I sighed as I watched. It would be easier not to be so annoyed if she weren't so very attractive. The senior boys of course, were hanging all around her.

It looked like there were 10 cars waiting in line to be washed, all under supervision by Bill the Italian teacher. Bob, the assistant principal, was by the group of students who were drying the cars and collecting money from the happy car owners. I mean, when in this day and age can you get a hand-washed and hand-dried car? At that moment, the school was dismissed, and a huge group of students came out of the building. Seniors who were honors students joined the Nut Squad washing cars. Everyone was yelling, singing, laughing, and joking. They were getting along fine. It was a nice view. I walked over to Bob.

"Hi Bob. How is it going?"

"Great, Maria. We made $300 this last hour."

"Wow! That's great." I looked at the line; another 10 cars were waiting. "Maybe the senior trip will pay for itself."

"I think it might. Any news yet on exactly who is doing these things in the school?"

I shook my head no.

"Well, I hope you figure it out soon. If I can help, just let me know."

I thought for a second. "There is this one little detail. Do you know if Booth took money out of the student account a lot?"

He frowned. "Yes, she did but I did not question her about it. Megan made a big withdrawal for her recently. Booth was always moving money around. I think she used it for some personal reasons and then returned it. At least I think that is what she did."

"Seems like there is a lot of money not accounted for."

Bob got a funny look on his face, as if something didn't make sense. He shook his head. "I don't know what to say. If I think of anything she said to me about funds I will get back to you."

"Thanks Bob. I have to go grill some food. Come and eat later." What was Bob thinking? Why that unusual look? "Tell everyone else to come too." I walked to Viola, who was looking at a $60,000 red Lexus that was getting washed. Ah, men!

"I am going to grill some hot dogs," I told Viola, who was talking to the Lexus owner about tires and interiors when I came over and made my grand announcement. I turned and walked off. I did not look to see if he was following me. Of course, he was following me. The cooks looked like they had the hot dogs under control. I was not needed at the grill.

I pulled up a chair and sat with a group of honors students for a change. After five minutes of discussing colleges and their golden futures I found myself bored silly. Give me the strange, community college bound Nut Squad any time! At least at that table, where Viola was sitting with them, they were discussing sports, bowling, guitars, songs and guitar playing, who was sleeping with who in their classes, who robbed the local Seven Eleven, etc. No wonder Viola had a very funny look on his face! At least he was having fun as I tried to bury a yawn. The discussion progressed to majors and minors at Yale. I was really envying Viola!

Then something very strange happened. Almost as a group; 10 of the honors students stood up and grossly threw up what looked like hot dogs right by their chairs. They threw up near the Nut Squad table too, and near Viola's feet. The boys in the Nut Squad jumped up and made various rude comments. Viola checked his Gucci's. I yelled for the school nurse.

Meanwhile as if a clock had been struck, 20 other seniors and sophomores threw up by their tables. It was a disgusting sight. I noticed none of the Nut Squad was sick. Strange! Viola, who had eaten three hot dogs, was not sick either. "Stop cooking and dishing out food!" I yelled at the kitchen staff. Some of them looked green in the face too. One head cooking staff member tried to make it to the inside of the school, perhaps to use a bathroom, where throwing up would be more private, when he lost his "cookies" by the door.

I didn't know who to deal with first, so I called for the assistant principals. None of them were at the tables yet. Some were in line with food, which they immediately threw out into the garbage bags. They came over to me in a group, Bob and Dickie with a few teachers in tow, Bill, Candy and Marge. Nan came too. I ordered Dickie to start manning the phones and calling parents to pick up their what I suspected were, food-poisoned children from the school immediately. He nodded.

I gave him Nan and Marge to help with calls. The others I asked to sit with the sick kids at a clean table and keep their eyes on them for any future illness. One of the few tables that was clean was where the Nut Squad was sitting. As if on cue they all moved and sat with me as if for protection. Still, none of them were sick. But they did look very nervous.

As I was calling for the nurse, Viola grabbed his phone and asked for backup. He walked over to the head chef Pierre and asked him to wrap up all the food for the police. He nodded and those of his crew who were not sick proceeded to wrap up the tons of leftover food on the serving tables.

183

A group of policemen arrived with the first parents, who'd come to collect their seniors or sophomores. A few of the parents stopped to tell me how unhappy they were with the school and with me. I tried to react favorably to them. Thank God there were only two weeks left in the school year before the seniors graduated! Hopefully after this year the superintendent would have another young principal in mind to take my place. Someone the parents would like better than me! I know I did not want this job anymore.

What looked like a medical team in white arrived. Maybe Viola had called in the EMT squad. They checked the remaining students out. They announced it looked like food poisoning and they took all the food to check in the lab. Viola wanted to know exactly what had happened. This could turn into another long day for me. I called Al and left a message on our phone stating that I was fine and what had happened. I told him to have dinner without me. The thought of food after this picnic was not a welcome idea! Viola came over just after I had finished my message.

"Let's go to your office. Also, please tell the teachers and assistant principals who are still here to join us when they are through. Tell Nan to keep them outside till we need them." He looked really unhappy. I was not happy either.

I signed to Nan, who came over. I explained to her what I wanted and asked her to tell the others. She nodded. Everyone on the staff was clearly upset. All of the murders, attempted murder, and now the food poisoning was making everyone very nervous about the future of their jobs and the future of the school. I was beginning to wonder what we would do if the murderer was not caught by the end of the school year. What about summer school? At this point I was going to cancel summer school if the person who did these things was not caught. I did not care what the superintendent had to say about his budget. I did not care about my job. I cared about the safety of the students and the staff. They came first in my mind.

Viola and I entered the office.

"What! No hotdog for me?" asked Smith.

Viola explained what had happened. Smith had not heard anything because Booth had almost soundproofed the office. It was really quiet with the door shut. I wondered how many private illegal conversations had gone on in this office. Why did Booth try to soundproof her office? What did she not want anyone outside to overhear?

Smith spoke up. "Megan has deposited the money back into the school fund."

I was beginning to dislike both the faculty whom I had worked with for years and the school funds.

26

Who Really Is in Charge of The Drug Ring?

The door to my office flew open. Dickie came in pulling Bill Mecca behind him. Bill was trying to break Dickie's hold and protesting loudly to be let go, but Dickie was stronger than he looked. Did it come from tackling students in hallways the few times he decided to do his job, or maybe from the running with Candy? Dickie threw him in a chair. Viola stood up. He looked at them both keenly as if ready to break them apart to prevent violence.

"I caught him opening a locker we emptied of drugs yesterday. He looked funny, and as the cops arrived at the picnic to see to all the sick students, I saw him sneak off, so I followed him. He knew the combination and opened a locker that was empty, just as I grabbed him." Dickie crossed his arms, stood over Bill and glared at him.

Viola turned to Bill. He stood over him too. "Well?"

Bill turned and looked at me. Then he looked at Viola. "Ok, you caught me. I was selling drugs in my classes to some of the girls who asked for them. But Booth knew it. She had set it up. Booth called girls in who were selling drugs in the school and told them from now on they would be reporting to her. The money was to go to her. She would pay them a salary weekly, if they followed the plan. They agreed. It gave the girls a steady income each week, which worked out better for them. The girls have told me that the salary they got was a lot of money, especially for these girls who came from poor homes.

It also gave her control of the money and where drugs were stored in the building and who could get to them. She called me in and told me that parents had reported things that had happened to some of the girl students in my room, and that unless I gave drugs to certain girls to sell, she would present the school board with charges about me. She said she was going to control the drugs in the school and I was going to be the middleman between her and the students.

That way, if anyone complained, I would be in trouble. No one would believe that she was in charge. She gloated over the situation. What could I do? I wanted to keep my job. I said yes. That's how the whole thing started." He went to stand up. Dickie pushed him down.

Viola spokes. "Did you kill Booth or Roberto?" Smith was taking notes rapidly at his side.

I was flabbergasted.

"I did not kill anyone."

"Did you set a bomb under Maria's car?"

"I can't even make a bomb," answered Bill, "so, no! Why would I want to harm Maria? She didn't know anything about me. I did not knock the newbie on the head, send notes to Maria, make bombs or kill anyone. I did not even put the pot in the lockers! Here!" He handed Viola a note. I read it over Viola's shoulder. It stated that Bill should look in lockers by the boy's bathroom, if he knew what was good for him. It was cut from letters that were pasted together from a newspaper. "Now I want a phone call and a lawyer. I am not saying anything more." Once he asked for a lawyer Viola stopped questioning him. Bill crossed his arms over his Armani suit coat and firmly closed his mouth. He turned and glared at Dickie strangely.

Viola took out his cell phone and called for backup. "Smith, read Mr. Mecca his rights."

I still could not believe it. Bill, of all people, part of a drug ring! I had never heard anyone read his or her rights in a principal's office. I could not believe this was happening. The superintendent was going to have a fit. Two cops in uniform came in as Smith finished. Smith went back to the table where she had been working. They cuffed Bill and led him away. As he left he turned to me and yelled that he wanted a sabbatical due to mental health issues. I doubted the superintendent would grant it. I wrote a note to check with him anyway.

I looked at Viola. "If you can, please get the names of those girls. I need to speak to them."

Viola smiled. "After I do."

Oh dear. It was going to be a long night in school. I called Al again and told him what had happened and not to wait up. Dickie stood over my desk. He was smiling. What a strange guy.

"Well," he said happily, "that ends that!"

Viola jumped in.

"It does not solve the murders."

Dickie frowned. "You don't think Mecca is lying, and he committed the murders anyway?"

Viola smiled as Dickie frowned. "No, I don't. But thank you for bringing in Mecca when you saw him." Viola in an untypical Viola gesture threw his arm around Dickie and led him to the door. He opened the door and almost threw him out. "Thanks again. You can go home now. We don't need you anymore. Have a great night!" Viola shut the door in Dickies' face as he opened his mouth. That ended that Dickie visit. The rest of the faculty was waiting outside with Nan. Viola looked at me. "Let's have them all in," he said.

I phoned Nan at her desk, and she had the faculty and assistant principals file in. It was a quiet group and there were not enough chairs for everyone. Many stood and leaned against the walls. I welcomed everyone. Then I explained about Mecca's involvement with the drug ring, being careful not to give too many details. I gave information about the students being involved. They had all seen Mecca taken out of the office dragged out cuffed, so explaining something was wrong was not a surprise. Some shook their heads in disbelief. Viola gave me a glance. How well we were beginning to know each other again. It was like we were starting to think alike.

"Now Detective Viola has a few things to say regarding the murders, the bombing of my car and the food poisoning this afternoon." I realized I had left out Tommie Newbie getting hit on the head. I just signaled to Viola to start. "We need information on anything strange happening in the school. Drug deals if you saw one, persons stealing supplies. Anyone who normally did not stay late at school you saw staying late. Report any money that was missing from your teaching or assistant principal accounts. Even the simplest thing you saw that struck you as odd may be of importance to us. Come into this office and let us know. You can call us for a private appointment. We want to solve the murders and get the school back on track to educating young minds. We need your help and the help of the students who you know notice things. Go home now; it has been a long day. Think. Come back in the morning and see us if you think of anything. Also, all after-school activities and trips are cancelled until these murders are solved and the police feel that students will be safe again here."

I glanced around the room, looking for anyone who looked guilty or as if they were hiding something from us. Everyone stared at Viola or at the floor in thought. No one looked like a murderer to me. No one was making eye contact with the person next to him or her. I wished everyone a good night and they filed out silently. I rose from my desk and said I was going home. Viola nodded. He got up to walk out to his car. Not much was discussed now. There was nothing to say. We knew a lot of facts but had no one to name as a murderer.

Smith drove me home and then took herself home. She said she would pick me up in the morning. Al was asleep when I got in. I sat in the living room for hours thinking through all the murders and the other happenings. I was getting a glimmer of an idea in the back of my head. I did not know yet whom to pin the murders on. We still needed proof, even if my idea was correct.

How would we get it? At this point it was 3 a.m. and I had to be at my desk by eight. I gave up and went to bed. Thinking I would not sleep, I immediately did. I had dreams about rich fatty foods that the whole faculty was eating in handfuls, and not one person was sick. Oh well. I wished that dream had been true.

27

Roberto

I got to my office at school, thinking a terrible thought. I had caught myself thinking this was "my" office. This meant that I was getting used to being principal. As I came into the outer office, there sitting in a chair was Jeff, from the Nut Squad. Oh boy, what a start to my day. Sitting next to Jeff was Mary, also of the Nut Squad. I waved at Nan and asked for coffee. Then I invited Jeff and Mary into my office. In my office Smith was on a computer and Viola was not to be seen. Oh well, up to now, I had enjoyed our morning coffee together.

Jeff and Mary stood until I came in and then threw themselves into chairs across from my desk. We all smiled at each other. They both reached into their backpacks and offered me gum. "Thanks," I said and stuck two pieces of gum in my mouth. A coffee and gum breakfast sounded about right today. Nan came in and handed Smith and me coffee. She smiled at the students and walked out. I waited for one of them to speak. Smith pulled up her chair and opened a notebook to take notes. Silence continued.

Finally, Jeff spoke. "Hey, like, Teach, er, I mean, principal. We were wondering if we could like know what happened to the money we found backstage. Was it drug money gathered by Mr. Mecca?" He and Mary looked at me.
"We think so, but we are not sure yet. Mr. Mecca has to answer questions that the police are asking him now." They continued to chew gum. I chewed mine. The students were thinking. I was thinking. Smith drank coffee The adults waited for the next question. The students stayed silent.

"Why do you want to know about the money?" I asked.

Mary jumped in. "Martha, Roberto's girlfriend, says that the cops are releasing Roberto from the freezer today. Roberto's parents called Martha and told her."

"The morgue," I state.

"Yeah, thanks, Teach, his parents don't have money to bury him proper in a Catholic Church funeral. They are ashamed to ask anyone for help, since they feel he must have done something bad to be killed like that." Mary looked at Jeff.

Jeff said, "so Teach, we were wondering could like that drug money sitting in the police station doin' nothing be used to bury Roberto and maybe have a small party at his parents' home, like they usually do when someone dies? It's very important to his parents. Can you do that Teach?" Both kids stared at me, awaiting an answer.

Poor Roberto's parents. In the mess of everything else that had happened at the school, I had not thought of a funeral for Roberto. I did not even know that the morgue was ready to release the body. I looked the two students in the eyes, "I will call Roberto's parents and have them come in today. We'll see what we can do for them. It was really wonderful of you both to let me know. Thank you. Please let the other students know that I will work on it today. Check with me at the end of the day and I'll give you an update on what's happening."

Mary and Jeff got up. "Thanks, Teach," they said. As they walked out of the office.

I called for Nan to come in. "Please call Roberto's parents and ask if they can come by here today to discuss Roberto's funeral with me." Nan nodded and walked out.

I reached for my purse, dug out my iPad, and looked up the phone number for the local Catholic Parish. I called the priest and told him that any expenses for the funeral of Roberto, the school would be happy to pay. I also looked up the phone number for one of my college buddies who ran a local funeral home. After spending time discussing old college pals and what they were doing, I explained about Roberto and his parents. He was quite sympathetic.

He told me to send the parents to him and he would get back to me with fair prices for the funeral. I thanked him warmly. He also said that when I knew the police were releasing Roberto's body he would arrange the pickup from the morgue. I thanked him again and we hung up with promises to have dinner together with our spouses soon.

Nan came in and said that Roberto's parents would be in to see me at one o'clock. I asked her to order lunch for them and for herself, Smith, Viola, and me at the same time. She said she would.

I turned to Smith. "I have to bury Roberto. His parents can't; they are very poor. Could we use any of Booth's funds for this that we're sure are school funds? Otherwise, I will need to take my own money out of the bank. The school board has emergency funds to pay for something like this and they would pay me back in the future. In this case, I can't even consult them, there is no time. Did Booth keep any of that money, or will I have to use my funds?"

Smith asked, "How much do you think you will need?"

"According to my friend at the funeral home, it would be about$5,000. Then we want a small party for the home and about $200 for the priest. We may also need money to buy a plot at the cemetery. I have to ask the parents about that. Some families have family plots. But they don't have a lot of money, so I don't know."

"So, you think about $8,000?"

"I think that would be more than enough."

Smith smiled at me. "Don't worry Booth had that in a separate account for School Emergency Funds. That money looks to be Ok and honestly made from school fundraisers."

"Great." The rest of the morning passed swiftly. Smith called the morgue; I recalled the funeral home and Roberto was moved from the morgue to the funeral home.

Roberto's parents arrived. They were very grateful that the school would help with the funeral. Their family had a plot in the local Catholic cemetery, so at least we would not have to buy a plot.

His father said, "I have $2,000 I was saving for Roberto to use for college. Now we will use it for his funeral." He looked me right in the eye as he

said it; I saw he was a very proud man. I nodded.
I gave them the name of my friend at the funeral
home. There was little talk after the discussion
about funds. As they were leaving Roberto's
mother took my hand. "Roberto loved you,
teacher. You will catch his killer for me". She
started to cry. I felt tears in my eyes.
    "Yes," I said softly.
    They left for the funeral home. What a terrible
thing it had to be to have to bury your own child.
    I sank into my desk chair, called the room
where the Nut Squad was, and asked the teacher
there explain to them I had taken care of the
funeral for Roberto. As soon as I had the date and
time, I would let them know. After the depressing
meeting with Roberto's parents, I really did not
want to see any students the rest of the day. Here
I am depressed as hell, and where was Viola?
Smith threw herself in the chair across from me.
"Maria, that was a lovely thing you just did."
    "Thanks, but I don't feel happy about any of this.
I really want us to catch this murderer. By the
way, where is Viola?"
    "Viola is talking to Mecca, trying find out the
names of the students he dealt with and sold
drugs to. He is also questioning him about the
murders to see if he was involved. Mecca has
gotten himself one of the most well-known
criminal lawyers in New York City. He is not
talking much. The DA is working on a deal for
him. Perhaps if the lawyers agree today, we will
have a little more information on what really

happened in the school." She sat back in the chair. She did not look happy.

I smiled at her. "Let's take a walk around the school together. Maybe as we walk past classrooms something will hit me as an idea." I hadn't realized the dismissal bells had rung. The soundproof walls did not let the bells ring loudly in the office. The halls had a strange echo in the empty school building.

Smith and I walked the top floor first. The echo was very noticeable to me. I had always thought that the halls missed the children when they went home. An unusual thought perhaps, but one I had believed most of my teaching career. On the top floor, there were no teachers or staff members. They had left for the day. We walked past doors that were locked and lights that were off in classrooms that were vacant. Late afternoon sunlight streamed through the hall windows. We went down to the second floor and walked some more.

I turned to Smith. "I think it is time to go home." When I got home, Al handed me a message from the funeral home. Roberto's parents were holding the funeral tomorrow afternoon. I called all the teachers and made it clear to them to inform the students and that all of them would be excused for the funeral at one o'clock at St. Mary's Church. Teachers and staff would be excused also, if they cared to attend. The students and faculty who did not attend would report to the auditorium with the school

aids. I called Smith and asked her to let Viola
know. I would be there and I thought they should
be there too. The police should be guarding my
students and the parents. There was a murderer
loose. Al and I had an early dinner and went to
bed. It was a depressing day.

28

Burying Roberto and almost someone else

Walking into the packed church for mass, I
noticed the faculty had sat together, perhaps for
protection. It was very unusual to see them
bunched up as a group. Too many personalities
that were so different were sitting in three pews.
Viola and Smith were standing at the back doors
as everyone filed past them on their way to seats.
Detective Perfect Viola smiled at me. Smith
nodded. Roberto's brother Jose whispered to me
that his Madre wanted me to sit with her. What
could I do? "Of course," I answered. I sat next to
Roberto's mother. She was in almost solid black
from head to toe. I could not see her face which
was covered by a veil.

The priest spoke about Roberto as a young
man. He seemed to have the details correct,
because Roberto's family started to cry all around
me. The priest spoke only about the good things
he knew of Roberto as a child. He did not
mention drugs or gangs. It was a sad scene.

After the mass, we walked out to the gravesite in back of the church. Roberto's brother walked with his mother and father, so I was free to stand close to the deep grave. The Nut Squad was carrying the coffin.

As they were ready to lower the coffin into the ground I heard a muffled scream from the dirt in the bottom of the grave. I yelled, "Hold it a minute!" The one thing that I had gotten the Nut Squad to learn was that if I yelled "Stop" they had to stop, or they would be writing essays for a week. They stopped. The coffin wavered a little at the abrupt stop but they manfully held on to it.

Viola in his beautiful suit (this one looked like a Ralph Lauren) came swiftly to my side. I was looking down at the bottom of the grave. I saw dirt. The scream I had heard did not happen again. Viola looked at me. "I heard something from the ground in the grave," I said facing him. Before he could say anything, I asked everyone for a minute of quiet. As soon as quiet reigned Viola and I both heard a muffled scream, and the dirt in the bottom of the grave started to move!

Viola threw me his suit jacket. Instinctively I caught it. I mean, why jump in a hole in the ground and get your designer jacket ruined? He jumped athletically into the grave like Valentino, a silent film star. Gosh, he was gorgeous! Using his hands, he dug at the dirt in the bottom.

There, tied up like a Christmas turkey, with what looked like an old gym sock in her mouth, lay Candy. A very messy Candy. Viola asked for a ladder to help him get her to the ground above. The gravediggers brought a ladder and helped him raise a turkey-tied Candy up to the ground. Roberto's mother fainted. A few of the women screamed when she was brought to the surface. Dickie screamed, "Candy!" He tried to run to her, but Viola ordered him back. Smith grabbed Dickie and held on to him. I was fascinated. Who would do such a thing to Candy?

Smith took out her cellphone and called for an ambulance and a team to the gravesite. Viola asked everyone to stand back from Candy, kneeling by her side he carefully started to remove the sock covering her mouth. He explained that she had to stay still until he could get a team to the church to record and remove the ropes on her. They could provide evidence for catching the person who had done this to her. Candy lay on the ground next to the grave still as a dead turkey. She looked even worse with her dirt-stained face and the white patches that were now free around her mouth and eyes.

The EMC team and the forensic people arrived rapidly. We were ordered to go back into the church with the coffin. They needed all our names and phone numbers. The funeral would have to wait. Roberto's mother wept, as her family led her back into the church. My Spanish was rusty, but I understood that she thought this was terrible.

We sat down again. This time I sat near the faculty. the Nut Squad, carrying Roberto, placed the coffin on the altar. They then sat in the back of the church whispering to each other. We waited for the police to take our information. I was very curious as to what was going on outside with Candy and the cops. But since I had been told to sit, I sat. Smith came looking for me. Viola wanted me to join the police and Candy.

I nearly ran outside to get away from the drama and sadness in the church. I brought Viola's suit jacket with me. He took it from my hands and put it back on. Candy was now with the ambulance EMT, who were taking her blood pressure and checking her out. Viola took my hand and drew me over to her. She looked as pale as a ghost. Her hair was totally covered in dirt and all of her makeup was gone. She normally was a very pretty girl, but not now.

Viola asked, "Do you know who did this to you?"

Candy had tears running down her face. She looked at me in shock. I took her hand to hold. She clung to it like a lifeline. "No. The last thing I remember I was walking to my car. It was parked in the back lot near the gym exit. It was about six o'clock. The last basketball activity had ended at six. I felt a hand go around my throat from the back and something heavy hit me over the head and I passed out. I turned around before I passed out, but all I saw was a figure in black with a mask on his head and gloves on his hands. All I can tell you is it was a man. I know he was a man because he was very tall and strong. He did not speak. I woke up to dirt all around me. I thought I wouldn't be able to breathe. I heard your group come to the gravesite and I started to scream as loud as I could. The next thing I knew was you digging me out of the ground. I would have been buried alive."

She started to cry again and the EMT person said that we had asked her enough for now. She needed to be moved to the hospital and checked out for any other injuries. She had a bump the size of an Easter egg on her head. Viola turned to Smith.

"I want you to go to the hospital with Candy and see if she remembers anything else once the doctor has checked her out. Also, please stay with her until I send an officer in a couple of hours to take your place."

Smith nodded. We climbed down from the ambulance and Smith climbed in. I told Candy I would stop by the hospital to see her as soon as I could get there. Dickie went for his car possibly to follow Candy to the hospital, but an officer stopped him. No one was allowed to leave the church grounds until the police interviewed them. Viola looked at me.

"She is lucky to be alive. She could have smothered. Maria, I want you to wait an hour or so and then go to the hospital. See if she will tell you anything that she did not say just now, then report back to me. I will go to the school tonight later and be in your office. I want to have a look at the gym and Candy's classroom and office.

Smith will join me there once I get an officer to stay with Candy. This may give us a break if we find something. Also, we have to figure out, why Candy? What does she know that someone does not want her to share?"

I did not have a clue. I had not expected this to happen to Candy. I had thought that she might be one of the ringleaders of the drug and money problems. I said nothing to Viola. I just nodded. He walked me to my car, told the police officers standing in the lot that I had permission to leave and sent me on my way to the hospital. As I drove away, in the rear-view mirror I saw Dickie walk over to Viola gesture to my car and start to argue with him. Dickie was determined to follow me. Viola just kept nodded his head no. I went home, explained to Al what had happened, changed my clothes and drove to the hospital.

29

The Truth will not set you free.

When I arrived at Candy's hospital room Smith was still there. Viola had not sent anyone to relieve her yet. Candy had her eyes closed and was sleeping. I whispered to Smith, "Do you want a break?" She nodded and walked out of the room.

She whispered as she walked past me, "I will bring you coffee." I nodded.

Once she left the room Candy cautiously opened one eye. She looked at me, sat up carefully, and spoke. "I was waiting for you to come. I'm glad you sent her for a walk. Maria, I am in big trouble.' She started to cry. I ran to the side of her bed and handed her a tissue and a glass of water. She drank thirstily and stopped crying. "I have two members of the faculty whom I am sleeping with at the same time," she announced in a whisper. I just nodded, I guessed that they were Dickie and Bill, but I wanted her to say so. "Dickie and Bill," She told me. This was no surprise. "I think one of them is trying to kill me."

I spoke finally. "Why?"

"With Bill, I knew about him selling drugs and the deal he had with Booth. She kind of told me. Booth said I could sell too, but I told her no. I am a gym teacher, for goodness sake; I don't let my dancers use drugs. And I finally got Bill to tell me the whole truth the day before Viola arrested him. Until that day, I knew nothing about the drug deal." She looked at me, her eyes wide and innocent, "I, of course, was not involved in the drugs."

I did not believe it for a second. She was in on the drug situation up to her beautiful baby blue eyes. I just nodded. I did not want her to stop talking.

"Dickie is jealous of Bill and me. He knew Bill was selling drugs; Booth told him to join Bill. Dickie demanded a cut from Booth to keep his mouth shut about the deals, but Booth said she would not give him anything. If he was not going to join Bill in selling, and he talked, she would fire him. Dickie was mad at Booth about this the last few weeks before her death. Booth told him she had records of all the money that he had used from the school fund to buy a new car and his new apartment. She said he had been cheating the custodial budget for years and saving that money to buy an apartment. She told him she had the proof in a safe place. He had a choice to make. He had to shut up about what was going on in school. He could join in and keep his job, or he could leave. He told me this right after she died. He also said he had not used any school funds for anything. I'm not sure if he did or didn't use school funds. I think he or Bill wants to kill me because I know too much."

I said, "but Bill is in jail."

She nodded, "But he could have asked one of his students to do this to me. They are extremely loyal to Bill. They would do something like this if he told them to; some of those girls really hate me. They think they are in love with Bill."

I wonder why they hate you I thought sarcastically. But I nodded again and said nothing.

She kept talking. "The stuff that has been happening in school, the murders, I don't know who did that." She leaned back and closed her eyes.

I leaned forward. "If you had to guess, why was Roberto killed?"

She opened her eyes; she looked angry. "Maria, you are the only one who seems not to realize that Roberto collected information by leaning against faculty bathroom doors and classrooms as he walked by. He came to the three of us one day as we sat in my dance classroom. He said he knew we were sleeping with each other. God knows I had tried to be careful and never had Dickie or Bill meet me at home. We never left from school together. Seems one-night Roberto followed Dickie and me to a hotel. He saw us check in at night and check out the next day. A few days later he followed Bill and me to the same hotel. He saw the same thing. He accused me of being a slut! *THIS KID FROM A POOR HOME WITH PARENTS WHO REALLY DON'T WORK ACCUSED ME!"* She shouted at me then she took a deep breath and continued her story.

"He said that if we did not give him money, he would see that the whole school would know what we were doing. He also told Bill that he knew about the drug ring. He didn't give us any details about Bill's plans, but he knew! I think one of them killed Roberto. What do I do now Maria?"

She stared at me. It was amazing that she really thought I could help her. I wanted her out of my

206

life and out of my school. I wanted all three of them out! If Booth had still been alive I would have kicked her out, too. Poor Roberto, he was just a dumb kid, a gang member, trying to make money by doing something that he thought was Ok. He was always eager to make money. What would his parents think when this came out? I looked at Candy. She made me sick. Had she had killed Booth or Roberto, or both of them? She stared at me. I was taking too long to think. "You should tell all of this to Smith, I think she will be easier for you to talk to than Viola. I can stay if you want me to." I smiled at her; it was painful to do so.

"Yes, please,"

Smith entered the room two coffee cups in her hands. I took one. Once Smith sat, I said, "Candy has something she wants to tell you." Smith handed me her coffee and pulled out a notebook. I sat through the whole sad, tale again. Smith read Candy her rights and cuffed her to the bed. She started to cry again. Smith then called Viola.

Twenty minutes later he entered the room rapidly. I could not take hearing the tale again. If I had to listen to it a third time, I might kill Candy myself. "I will be in the waiting room," I said and walked out. I sat in the waiting room down the hall and I started to drink my coffee. My head was spinning with Candy's story. Seemed like we had a choice of three murderers. I could not see Bill doing it, he did not have the backbone. Bill seemed too nice to kill someone.

I could see him sleeping with Candy. I could see him selling drugs, but I could not see him killing anyone. Dickie I could see doing anything, he was such slime. Dickie's wife was home with little children, the youngest only six months old. And Dickie was cheating with Candy? Candy was beyond slime. She could have murdered them too. But something in the back of my head was bothering me. Could I see them in the basement chasing me? Could I see them stabbing a person to death? Why poison the food at the car wash? Why hit the newbie principal over the head? He did not know about the drug ring.

Something else was at work here; that is what bothered me as I sat and drank the coffee. The idea I had had as a glimmer of an answer would not work now. Not since Candy was thrown into a grave. That was a very strange thing to do. Why did the killer not just kill her? Why leave her to tell a story in which she could say she saw the person who threw her in the grave? Why was Candy still alive?

Viola came out of Candy's room and joined me on the lumpy waiting room sofa. He said nothing for a few minutes.

"Maria, thank you for getting her to confess her story. But I am not sure why the killer, if it was the killer who put her in the grave, would leave her alive. It is quite a chance for a killer to take."

"I agree. I was sitting here thinking the same thing. Why is Candy still alive? I feel there is something else going on here. But at least now you have something on slimy Dickie to ask him about. I can't wait to know what he says."

"Dickie said when you drove away to follow Candy to the hospital that he was going to come right over to see her. I told him she was under police guard and he was welcome to sit in the room with a cop present. His face turned red, and he walked away from me. I hope he does show up, so I don't have to track him down."

What could I say? I hoped Dickie showed up too. And as if on cue in a play, he walked past us heading for Candy's room. There was a tall man in a suit carrying a briefcase in back of him. It looked to me as if Dickie had lawyered up. Viola jumped up and ran after him. I rose, and at a gentler pace, and followed. When Dickie hit the door of Candy's room, the screaming started.

She had more voice than I ever gave her credit for. Injured as she was, she could still really yell at Dickie. "What are you doing here? Are you a fool?"

Dickie, who was standing as close to her bed as Smith would let him, yelled back, "I was worried about you! I brought you a lawyer, Mr. Raj."

"How nice!" she said nastily. "So very nice of you to think of me after you tried to kill me! Get out!"

Dickie turned white as a sheet. "I did not try to kill you! Do you remember who did?"

Candy stopped talking over him. She took a deep breath, "If it wasn't you maybe it was Bill.

I was walking to my car and the next thing is I am buried in a grave. I did not see who did it!"

"Honey. You forget since you got hit on the head, maybe, that Bill is in jail."

Candy narrowed her beautiful baby blues and glared at him. "I know that, stupid! He could have hired someone! Or maybe you hired someone! Thanks for the lawyer. He can stay. You," she paused for effect, pointing at Dickie, "get out!" Dickie started for the door. Viola grabbed him. Mr. Raj stepped up next to Viola's expensive lapels. "Is my client under arrest?"

"Which one?" asked Viola, Dickie and Candy at the same time.

Mr. Raj looked confused. The three of them glanced at each other. Viola spoke first.

He told Dickie he was under arrest for selling drugs to minors and other charges that he needed to think about downtown. Dickie told Mr. Raj to stay with Candy as Smith frog- marched him out of the room, into the hall, in handcuffs. What a gentlemen Dickie was! A cop in uniform met Smith and left with Dickie.

Smith was relieved of the job of guarding Candy. Viola posted a plain-clothes cop with Candy and Raj and told the cop he would be relieved at midnight. The cop was ordered not to leave Candy alone, as there was a murderer loose. Candy thanked Viola and, I swear, batted her eyes at him. Viola nodded at me and waved me ahead of him to the door.

After we cleared the room. He asked, "Want to go to the station with me? You can't sit in on the interview with Dickie, but you can listen in the glass booth. I will make you a temporary deputy down in the station. Maybe we will finally get some answers."

What girl could refuse such a proposal? Made an assistant deputy? It was almost like a date. I was too excited to answer and just nodded as Viola the Hunk and I went arm in arm to the patrol car. I really hoped we would learn about who killed poor Roberto. Viola opened the car of the car, helped me in, and we took off at blinding speed, as blinding as it gets on city streets in Queens.

30

Confessions of an Assistant Principal

We arrived in the police station in Forest Hills and Smith was there at the door. "They are processing him now, sir, and will have him in Room B. He has a lawyer with him. Seems Candy and Raj got some female lawyer over here first thing."

Viola thanked Smith and led me into his office, where he really did swear me in as temporary deputy. But he would not give me a gun. I asked: he said no. What a poop! Then he led me to where Smith was sitting, looking through a glass wall at Dickie and his lawyer. They had their heads very close together and appeared to be whispering. We could hear the whispering over the speakers in the wall above our heads. We couldn't tell what they were saying. Viola opened the door and entered the room. He sat. The whispering stopped.

"Dickie, do you have anything you would like to tell me?"

Dickie looked around the room wide eyed as if in panic. "Like what?"

"Did you throw Candy into an open grave recently?"

"No, of course not! I love her. If she would dump Bill, I would divorce my wife and marry her!"

Oh Boy. That poor woman, Dickie's wife, with those tiny children.

"So, if you did not throw her into the grave, who did?"

Dickie stared at Viola with his mouth open. Not the best of looks for him.

The lawyer spoke up, "You don't have to answer him."

Dickie glanced at her, like he had forgotten she was there with him. He looked panicked. "No, it's ok, I think maybe Bill planned it. Because maybe he's afraid, about the drug thing that's going on in school. Maybe he is afraid Candy will come to you and talk."

"So, "Viola said softly, "what about the drug thing?"

The lawyer spoke again. "No! You don't have to answer that either!"

Dickie waved her off. "Candy talked. How could I get in any deeper trouble than I am already?"

It was the lawyer's turn to look amazed. Dickie was not the brightest egg.

"See, we were short of funds because we were not getting good raises the last 10 years or so."

My God! This had been going on for 10 years!

"It started as a joke really; could we sell a little pot to the students on the side? Seems Bill and Candy knew dealers that were their friends and Bill always got along with students who were girls. I mean, really, really, really get along, if you get my meaning."

Dickie grinned at Viola. Viola grinned at Dickie.

Just one of the boys I thought. Yeek!

"So, we thought, why not? Let's start something and see how it goes. But I didn't know Booth was into it and wanted a cut of the profits. She said she knew drug dealers who would give her cut rates on the drugs due to demand. Since we were in a school, the dealers seemed to think we would sell more drugs. We could make more money faster. She wanted to take control of everything and give us a cut. She said if we didn't play along she would expose us as drug dealers to minors and expose our three-way affair. We went along with her plan.

I think, everyone was happy with the new arrangement. That is, until Booth was killed. We got drugs after hours from her. Bill and his groupies sold them after school, while Bill was tutoring. The tutoring thing was a great cover for all of us; many students needed tutoring. We could sell a lot of drugs during tutoring sessions, and no one would be the wiser. Candy sold with me in the locker rooms after practices. Except she wouldn't sell drugs to her dance students. Don't ask me why. Maybe because she always wanted to be a professional dancer. Dancers can't be on drugs. We all made extra money.

Bill caught Roberto listening in the doorway outside Candy's room one day. We started to pay him off so much a month, but only a small amount. Nobody was supposed to get hurt. Then he turned up dead too. I don't know who killed anyone. I mean, why kill anyone? We were making money. The murders don't make sense to me. Lock me up. I really have nothing more to say to you."

Dickie closed him mouth and his lawyer asked for charges.

Viola explained that Dickie would see a judge in a few days. Right now, he would be held for murder, attempted murder, and drug dealing with minors. A cop took Dickie to wherever alleged criminals went next. Smith smiled at me and walked out of the room. Viola left the room I was observing and Dickie's lawyer walked out after him.

I thought that this did not seem to be working out. We still did not know who murdered

Roberto or Booth. I sat for a while and thought. Then it hit me. The answer had to be somewhere in the school in Booth's office or somewhere in the offices. Now was a perfect time to check. There was no one at school. It was early evening, not yet dark out, a beautiful June day. It would not be dark for a few hours yet. It was a perfect time to snoop around.

I stopped myself from thinking that way. I was the principal! I had a perfect right to check out people's offices and look around. I could snoop all I wanted and no one could stop me. I wanted to solve these murders even if it killed me! I grabbed my purse and headed for the door.

Outside the police station stood an empty cab. I hopped in not believing my luck. The nice cabby took me back to school and promised to return in an hour and pick me up. I gave him my cellphone number and turned the cellphone on. I did not keep it on during work hours for fear it would ring in a classroom. I had never learned how to put it on mute and vibrate. I walked into the school.

31

Was it Colonel Mustard in the Library with a Wrench?
The Final Clues Fall in Place.

I went to my office and sat for a few minutes. It was quiet and dark. I put on all the lights, and saw that my answering machine had a message. It was from Roberto's father. They were burying Roberto in the morning at a private family funeral. They were not doing a party at the house and they didn't want anyone coming by, after what had happened at the church yesterday. I could understand that. I quickly wrote a memo to my assistant principals telling them the situation, and asking them to explain it to the students. I then threw the switches to light all the hallways in the school. I didn't plan to walk around a dark building ever again. It was deadly quiet. I thought about where to start and I decided to do Dickie's office in the basement first.

Down the stairs I went. And with keys in hand and a cellphone in my pocket I entered Dickie's inner kingdom. I went to his desk. His computer, had been taken by Viola, I opened all his drawers and read through his files. There was nothing there about the drug ring. I took some files that needed further reading to read in my office. I could not get through everything in one night.

Next, I checked out Bill's classroom and his files. No luck there either, I did find an interesting collection of semi-nude senior girls in his drawers. Oh Boy, I couldn't believe it. I gathered up files from his desk and walked them down to my office, too. I took the photos to show to the girls' parents.

I then made my third trip down to Candy's office in the gym. I had forgotten about her gym office until I was in the cab tonight. In the back of her dusty file drawers I found a little red leather notebook. Inside were hand written lists of initials in code. What was it with these codebooks? Were we in a spy movie? Was James Bond going to make an appearance? How did these people learn codes? Was it Booth who taught them? Amounts of what looked like funds were written next to the codes. How appropriate a red notebook for a list, how female of her. At least these initials looked like they might belong to names. Probably names of students.

I could not figure out the initials to match any of the students that I knew off the top of my head. It was getting late and I decided my cab would be outside soon. I took the book, stuffed it into my inside jacket pocket over my heart. I did not want to lose it before I showed it to Viola. I took Candy's files and headed for the door to climb to my office.

It was then I got the feeling that I was not alone in the basement. Oh. no! Not again! I heard a creak down the hall. I fled up the stairs as fast as my sneakers would take me and down the hall to my office. I locked my office door.

But then I realized that whoever this was, they had keys to the whole building. I was sure they would be able to open my office door. I dropped the files from Candy on my desk and opened one of the back doors of my office.

The outside lights automatically came on, lighting the field. The door led to the student's baseball field and I grabbed a bat left lying on the ground. I would have to have a word about gym equipment lying around on the field. Students needed to be taught to pick up after themselves. What was I saying? Who cared about that now? I needed a weapon! If I lived through this, I would have a talk about gym equipment. I held the bat firmly in my hand and reached for the phone in my pocket. I speed-dialed Viola's number.

Smith picked up. Why was I not surprised? Well, no time to figure out why Smith and Viola were always together, even at night. A mad killer was after me! Who knew what was going on between them? Why was I wondering about that now?

"Hello, Maria, answer please!" Smith said firmly. Ah, the magic of Caller ID.

"I'm on the baseball field. Come! Help!" I whispered into the phone. I did not want the insane killer to hear me. The next voice I heard barking at me was Viola. Boy, did he sound steamed. I wondered with a sense of dismay what romantic scene I had interrupted. Why were these two always together? I had a very vivid imagination.

"*What baseball field?*" he yelled. Really, we needed to speak about his tone with me when I saw, *if*, I saw him next.

"The school baseball field," I whispered. "Someone is here and they are following me. Hurry! I'm armed with a baseball bat, but hurry!" I jammed the phone back into my pocket when the talking at the other end started. I did not have time for a long conversation with Viola. I just heard my office door open and I turned to face it from the pitcher's mound. All I could see was a huge black shape dressed in a cape from head to toe in black exiting my door. It wore a black mask like a ski mask covering its face. It was heading for me! I ran to the batting cage.

Our school batting cage was designed with two doors, one for the batter and one for the coach, in case there was a problem with the ball machines. I am not a baseball expert, but I planned to lead our friendly neighborhood killer into the batting cage and practice my batting on his/her head! The one sport I knew well from my college days was hitting a hard, fast ball. Also, as I am getting older I've found batting an excellent place for me to get some exercise. Into the cage I ran and locked the door away from the ball machine. Then there was only one entrance into the cage, unless the killer had gym keys. If he/she had gym keys I was cooked. I started the ball machine, locked it into the play mode with a gym key, and prayed there were enough balls in it to hit until the police arrived. How many balls were in a hopper? I couldn't think about that now.

The person in black was whispering my name "Maria, Maria," as he/she opened the cage. The creepy murderer apparently did not have gym keys, as he/she came in the one unlocked entrance, thank goodness! Perfect. I would have a live target! I picked off a ball and hit it hard to the head of the cloak. The murderer ducked and stepped a foot closer. But another ball immediately flew out and I hit it again, this time striking the person full in the body. I heard a sharp intake of breath, but the steps kept coming closer. I aimed the next one down in the body, hoping to hit a vital reproduction area.

I missed. I guess I hit a leg for the villain yelped and limped forward. I hope I broke a knee. Then I heard cop cars in the distance, so did the person in black.

The person turned and looked at the cop lights coming down the road. He/she removed what looked like a wrench, from his/her clothing and threw it at my head! It was a fast throw and I was not looking for it, I was just hitting balls at the thing in black as fast as I could. The wrench gazed my head. I started to bleed. The sirens got closer. The villain turned and ran limping for the car parking lot. I sat on the ground.

Al was not going to be happy about another visit to the hospital. All I could think about before I blacked out was the Clue game and Colonel Mustard with a Wrench. That was my last thought until I woke up in a hospital with Al again holding my hand.

32

Home from The Hospital With the Little Red Leather Book

I was released from the hospital into Al's care the next morning. I had a head wound, but luckily nothing serious. I had met the cute doctor again too, but I still did not get his name, as I was doped up from the head wound.

Anyway, Al took me home, where I was ordered to the couch. He said Viola was angry at me for trying to play detective, and he was angry at me and I was not to go anywhere alone from now on until the killer was caught. I said nothing, nodded my head in agreement (which really hurt to shake) and sat on the couch for a day, pretending I was following instructions. I called the school to say I would not be in, and that Megan, the math assistant principal, was in charge until I got back. Megan had a principal certificate. Frankly, it was hard to choose who to put in charge of the school, since all the assistant principals were suspects.

The next day Al left early in the morning, he had to go out of town to a fish fair in New Jersey. I dressed, put a hat over my bandaged head and took a cab to school, since it seemed my husband had hidden all the car keys in the house! Can you believe he did not trust his own wife to obey instructions? I did not leave a note, since he did not trust me and I knew he would be back late. I planned on leaving school on time. I wanted to see who on the staff was limping and show Viola and Smith the red leather book. It had still been in my jacket pocket when I got home from the hospital. I was surprised Viola had not searched my clothes while I was in my hospital bed. Since no one trusted me anymore.

Al had told me that Viola ran across the baseball field ahead of his men, and he picked me up and carried me to the ambulance himself. He had ridden with me to the hospital! I wondered if he held my hand? I wished I had been awake for the rescue. Getting carried off the field by the Hunk sounded wonderful and romantic. He had called Al when he got to the hospital. What a prince! I could not wait to thank him.

I arrived at school and went straight to my office hoping Smith or Viola was there. Nan greeted me and immediately brought coffee to my desk. She informed me that the superintendent had replaced Candy, Bill and Dickie this morning with temporary help from his own office, until I could hire replacements for the next school year.

I tried not to make a face. I strongly doubted that after this mess of murders and drug use was straightened out, I would even think about being a principal again. Who was he kidding? Did he really think I wanted this job forever? If I made it

222

to the end of June without getting murdered I would be lucky at this rate!

I sipped my coffee and then noticed that Smith was standing at my desk, gazing at me with her mouth open. It was not a pleasant look. I gestured her to a seat, she went, got her coffee and sat. Then she spoke.

"Maria. I will not let you go anywhere without me from now on."

Another person was mad at me. Well, there must be a long line of them.

"Look, I had an idea, and I acted on it. I know that was not the best thing to do. And next time I will bring you with me. Meanwhile, I found this book buried in Candy's desk. Maybe together we can figure it out."

She took it from me and put it on the desk without opening it. That was self-control. She continued as if I had not spoken. "Viola was really upset to find you knocked out on the baseball field. He said it was my fault for not being with you all the time. I don't want my boss mad at me because you did something silly like go it alone and without letting me know. Are we clear?"

"Yes." More than clear. Viola got mad at her, over little old me? Well, who would have thought it? Maybe they were not a couple, and the idea that they were was just my romantic nature.

She then picked up the book and started reading. In a minute she looked up frowning. I handed her a yearbook from my desk. "You could try to match the initials to kids in the yearbook. Maybe if we interview enough of them, someone saw something. Or they saw someone else besides Dickie, Candy and Bill."

I had tried yesterday when I was on the couch to match names with initials, but my mind was foggy from the hit. I decided to see what Smith came up with. I finished my coffee. Just as I put the cup down Viola came into the office.

He had an amazed look on his face. I guess he could not believe I was back at my desk. He came around the desk and hugged me! Smith was engrossed in the yearbook and the red leather book. She did not look up.

He glanced at her. I glanced at her. Smith looked up at us both. "Maria found this," she said. He took the red leather book and flipped through it. Smith explained my idea. He nodded.

"See you later." I headed toward the door. I had things to do.

Viola said, "No, you don't!" and ran to the door to block me from exiting.

I glared at him.

"Before you go anywhere, one of us goes with you. Also, I want a description of this maniac who was after you last night. You tried to talk to me at the hospital, but you were too drugged."

"He/she was tall, about six feet in height. Dressed in black from head to toe. A cloak of black blocked me from seeing if it was a tall man or a woman. I think it stole the Hamlet cloaks from backstage before it painted the rest of them green. You might have someone check that. I had 15 black cloaks for the show and I'm sure I do not have 15 backstage now, especially since they were painted. I think it moved like a man, but I am not sure about that. Those Hamlet cloaks are bulky and it is hard to tell exactly. It was fast on its feet and whispered in that strange voice which told me nothing about its gender. I hit it twice. What I want to do today, before Al gets home and kills me for leaving the house, is to assemble the faculty and staff in the auditorium at 10 o'clock. Nan can organize the meeting for me. The students will have to report to the student cafeteria for a movie with the school aids. That way, everyone on the faculty can report to the auditorium without worrying about the students. We can introduce the two new teachers and new assistant principal and see if anyone is limping as they come into the auditorium. Maybe you can station some of the police in the auditorium while I do this, and we can catch someone. What do you say?"

He removed his hands from the doorframe and nodded. He looked at me with a smile. "Sounds like a great plan, Maria. Don't go farther than Nan's desk, though."

I walked out into Nan's office, told her the plan and she sent student runners to every room in the building to tell the faculty. She then made an announcement over the PA, in case any of the student runners had missed a faculty member.

No one could say they weren't told about the meeting, it was covered. It was 9 o'clock. I asked for another coffee and two aspirins. I went back to my desk, Viola sat with Smith and looked at the code book. They started researching initials together using the yearbook. I closed my eyes after the aspirin and took a nap.

33

Doesn't Every Teacher Love a Faculty Meeting?

As I walked to the front of the auditorium, I wondered if the faculty was secretly voting on how long I would last. Just like we had voted on Tommie Newbie. I looked right and left, then ordered everyone by name to a different corner of the auditorium. I told them it was for a meet and greet. They had one minute to find out about a hobby of someone in their group that they had never spoken to before. I mixed up teachers and assistant principals. One by one the groups formed. Everyone walked to a group. No one limped or showed any discomfort.

I checked the attendance list as I called people into groups; no one was absent either. I made them all return to their chairs after a few minutes for yakking. Then I made them report to the room. It took forever. Everyone had to come up front and report. More yak yak yak. I was concentrating on finding the limper, but no luck. It looked like no one had been hit in the leg with my fast ball. I couldn't find the murderer this way.

I introduced the new faculty members and assistant principal then let them go early to their next class and got a round of applause for doing that. But no one stood out as a villain. I was not feeling well by this time. I sank into a chair in the front row. The police came up to me. Viola asked if I wanted to go home. Of course, I did. I wanted the killer more than I wanted to go home, but I decided I could not do anything more today. I went home. Smith drove me.

34

Studying the Little Red Leather Book and Making a Night Raid Plan

I woke up the next morning at nine! I was starving! Al had let me sleep through the previous afternoon and evening. I decided to give my husband a break and stay home. I called the school and put Megan in charge as principal for the day again. I had a ton of sick days in my sick bank.

Tonight, was Al's Fish Meeting Night. Al would leave around 5 to meet his buddies for dinner and then the meeting would go till 11 p.m. or so. I would have lots of time at the school this evening. I planned to check out the school after hours. Since the *KILLER* seemed to like after-school hours, I decided *I* would learn to like them too. Maybe tonight I could finally nail him or her!

The message light was blinking. It was from Viola. He said they had four of the kids from the list in the red leather book at the police station with their parents this morning. They had all brought lawyers. Seemed they were all users of the evil weed. He would call me at home today if he learned anything else. I wondered whether I knew the four students and I hoped none of them were the Nut Squad. I took my copy of the red leather notebook, which I had copied on our home Xerox machine before I gave it to Smith, took a yearbook and sat down to figure out more names. If Smith and Viola could do it, I could do it! I sat there staring at initials. The next thing I heard was a ringing phone. I had fallen asleep over the books. It was Viola.

"Hi Maria, how are you feeling?"

"Great!" I answered brightly. He did not need to know I had slept away half the day! It was four o'clock. "Who are the students you spoke to?"

"Tommy Smith, Vicki Gearing, Nick Reterino, and Cathy Hurry. "

Boy, four of the senior honors students. What was going on in my school? I said nothing and waited for Viola to continue.

"Seems they brought weed from Candy, Dickie and Bill. One of them mentioned they saw Bob outside the room when they left. But no one saw him in the classroom when the selling was going on. How well do you know Bob?"

"I know him pretty well. He is a good assistant principal, and except for his half-truths about how Booth was treating him, I can't see him doing this. He could retire tomorrow, or move to another school, where they would love to have him."

"Maybe he was planning to improve his retirement funds," Viola said.

I chuckled.

"Or maybe Booth pushed him into it," Viola continued.

"No, I don't think so. Besides you don't have a witness that said that Bob was seen in the room with the students while the drug deals were going on. Right?"

"Right. But I still would like to check him out in the next few days. Maybe we can meet in your office? When are you coming back to work?"

I paused. I was going into the school tonight, but Viola would spoil my plans. "Tomorrow I will be in by ten," I replied. That way, if I were in school late without connecting with the killer, I did not have to drag in early the next day.

"Good, Maria, I will see you then. Rest up."

I opened my mouth to reply, but he had hung up on me! I was sitting there on the couch thinking when Al came home to change and get to his meeting. He said he was proud of me for staying home and taking care of myself. I smiled at him, told him he looked great, kissed, and waved to him, as he left for the Fish Club. One problem solved. As soon as I was sure he was gone I threw on some jeans, an old shirt and some sneakers. No one would be in the building to see how I was dressed. Unless they were sneaking around and not supposed to be in the building anyway. And that's what I was hoping. I was hoping to catch someone. I wore comfortable clothes in case I had to flee a villain again. No use running for help in one-inch heels! Besides, I could hit a better baseball in sneakers if I had to again!

I left Al a note. I marched out to a waiting cab. In case I did not come home, someone would know where I was. Al would be very unhappy with me, but he would send help. Then he would yell at Viola and me. By the time I had finished thinking about getting to school, I was there. I went into my office and locked myself in.

Something was bothering me, something about Bob. He had had a funny expression on his face at the car wash when I was talking to him. I wish I could remember what we had talked about, but my memory was a blank. Getting hit on the head did not help. But something about our conversation was really bothering me.

Could Bob be the Mastermind? I could not believe it about him. He loved his job. The faculty all looked up to him. Then, I realized that Bob never really did things like faculty parties. He was not an attendee except at my play, and when I invited him to cast parties he always had something else to do. He went to sports, but never out for a pizza party afterwards with the students. He did the job he was meant to do, but he did not do anything else. I suddenly wondered if he had any friends among the staff. Did I know anything about his life outside of school? Was anyone ever invited to his home? I did not know of anyone on the English faculty who said they had been to his home or met his family. And how come none of us had noticed that we never saw him outside school? How strange is that? How strange was Bob?

I was thinking all this when something upstairs bounced on my ceiling with a loud thump. I hoped it was a cop or security person, but I doubted it. I got a bottle of water from my refrigerator and drank it as I waited to see if I heard anything else. Sure enough, five minutes and half a bottle of water later, I heard another thump. I got goose bumps on my arms. I knew I would have to see what was happening upstairs.

The thought of exploring on my own, even after my brave ideas while at home, did not excite me, but I knew I had to go look. I took the bottle of water, my phone, and a big umbrella covered with dust that Booth had hidden behind one office door with me. At least I could club someone with a dusty umbrella and give him or her an allergy attack. I locked my office door behind me, though at this point the murderer had a key to every room, straightened up resolvedly and marched to the nearby stairs. There was no way I was meeting a crazy person in the elevator. At least on a stairway I could try to get away from them. I walked up to the second floor. It was dark but I didn't care if the killer knew someone else was in the building. I did not think they would be scared of meeting anyone, but I wanted them to know they were not alone. Did this make sense? No, but I did not want to walk around in the dark.

I keyed on the lights on the second floor and started to walk it, determined to check every room. And I did, well, at least I started to, when I found the unconscious cop in Room 203, which was the second-floor faculty lounge. I tried to wake him up, but he was really out. Someone had forcefully knocked him on the back of the head. A baseball bat was next to him covered in blood. I grabbed the tablecloth from the faculty table and wrapped it around his head. I called Viola's number direct. I had put him on my speed dial, thinking I might need it in the future. He picked up on the first ring.

"Maria? Where are you? Are you home?"
I decided not to clue him in so fast as to my location. He would tell me to wait in this room till the police arrived. This was no time for a chat.

"I am at school."
He started to yell.
"There is a knocked-out cop at my feet."

He stopped yelling at me, drew a breath, and asked as if he were talking through clenched teeth, "Where?"

"If you stop yelling I will tell you. I am in Room 203. I left the back door in my office unlocked in case you had to come in. It's the one on the baseball field, but I guess you could break in the front door. I am going to check the rest of the building. The security guard is missing too. Did you leave any other cops here?"

He hissed at me. "Maria, do not move from that room!"

I knew he would say that.

I hung up and put the phone on Vibrate. I had finally figured out Vibrate while I was home today.

I knew he would call back. The phone started to vibrate. But I was going to find out who hit the cop over the head, the location of the guard, and where the thumps were coming from.

I was the principal!

I started down the hall. I checked all the rooms and found nothing. Taking a deep breath, I walked up to the third floor. I found the lights on there. Then I heard police sirens turning into the school driveway. I decided to skip the rooms and go straight to Bob's office. I had to know if all of this had something to do with Bob.

35

My Last Conversation with Bob

Bob's office lights were on. I knocked. He
called, "Come in!" I entered the spider's web. He
was sitting at his desk. He was dressed in black.
A cloak from my play was draped over the
visitor's chair. He smiled at me! I hoped I could
keep him here till the police hit the third floor. I
knew Viola would look for me.

I sat down on the cloak. He pulled out a
thermos and poured us each a cup of tea. He had
these dainty china teacups that he always used on
his desk. They were teacups that women
collected. It never struck me as odd before that he
should have teacups like that on his desk till now.
Why did he have such delicate cups?

I took a cup and put it next to me on a corner
of the desk near the dusty umbrella. I then
noticed the top of his desk had about 50 plastic
packets and what looked like oregano in each
one. That pushed all thoughts of Bob's teacups
out of my head. I realized this was pot. He
sipped the tea. After he sipped the tea, I assumed
it was safe. I sipped the tea. It was nice and
warm. He smiled wider.

"Maria, you figured it out, haven't you?"
I frowned at him. "Figured what out?"
He smiled.

That smile was making me nervous. I gestured to his desk. "I see that you have some herbs there."

He laughed. "Ah, Maria, still innocent about high school students, are we?" He paused for effect. I realized he was just waiting for an audience. I sat back. I could play audience; I did it a lot when watching the students act.

"This is POT!" he yelled.

I nearly dropped the teacup. I had to keep him talking. I was listening to hear police on the third floor. I heard nothing.

"I realize that now, Bob. Thank you for telling me. Were you involved with Candy and Bill in selling?"

He laughed out loud. "Candy and Bill? No. They worked for Booth. We all worked for Booth, until I got sick of reporting to Booth. Then someone killed her. Booth, Booth," he got up and crossed to sit on the edge of his desk near me.

A little too close, I thought. I had no room to move anywhere unless I went out the door. If I lived through tonight the next English assistant principal would have to have a bigger office. In case the next was as nutty as this one, at least I would have room to move away.

"Booth, I hated Booth. Did you know that Maria?" He looked at me. His knee was touching mine. I nodded. What could I say? I had to keep him talking. Someone must be on the way to the third floor by now.

"We all disliked Booth," I said.

"But did you kill her?" He asked, smiling very widely.

"Did you?" I asked.

I was beginning to see double. What was in the tea? He drank it first! Had he drugged me somehow? He must have lined my cup with something maybe a knock-out drug. He laughed. That was the last thing I remembered. I woke up on stage. Hanging from the fly-walks above the stage. My head was down, my feet up and a strange cloaked figure was below me. It was a long way down, about 25 feet, and I was really tied up. I felt like a trussed turkey. I could not move. "Bob, is that you?"

I then noticed there was a very bloody body on the stage in a uniform; I guessed it was the school security guard. He was not moving. Was he dead?

"Maria, so glad you could join us. I have to tell someone and since this will be the last time you get to listen to me, or anyone else, I will tell you everything." He opened the cloak, uncovered his face, and threw out his hands. It was Bob. He had the remote control for the raising and lowering of the fly in his hands. This was not a good sign for me. It he hit Down, I would be part of the stage floor rather quickly. Where was hunky Detective Joe Viola? Right now, I'd even be happy to see Smith.

"So, Bob, did you kill Booth?" I had to keep him talking.

"Yes, I killed her. She was a nasty woman who tried to control me. She hated my ideas for the building. She refused to even buy our department new books. She hated the ideas for the drug money; she wanted to keep most of it for herself. She did nothing! Sat in her office, collected nasty secrets about people and used them to make these people part of her drug ring. She hated all of us, Candy, Dickie, Bill, and me. Of course, the three of them were fools. Candy Dickie and Bill all having sex together *YECK!*

And then stupid, stupid Roberto caught them. I should have killed the 3 of them instead of Roberto. But Roberto wanted money. I was sick of giving part of my money to others who were not involved in the drug ring. No! He had to go. I decided then to poison Candy, Dickie and Bill and the students at the carwash. I wanted the drug ring for myself. I was tired of sharing anything."

"Why did you want to kill the students?" I asked.

"I never teach classes, and no one ever wondered why. It was because I *hate* the students. Too bad some of them did not die, always sneaking around listening to conversations walking everywhere without supervision, asking stupid questions. Figured if they had died, you would have a lot of explaining to do."

My skin crawled to hear an educator talk so coldly about murdering students. I tried to keeping loosening the ropes around me, but nothing was moving. And if I did get free, what would I do? I would fall on the stage floor and die.

"I think after I finish here tonight, I will go see Candy in the hospital. She needs to die. She is such a slut. She always thought she was smarter than me."

What could I say to keep him talking? "Tell me, how did you kill Booth so easily? There was no disturbance in the office when I got there that morning. She was just dead." I was trying to compliment him to keep him talking.

Suddenly, in the back, I saw one of the auditorium doors quietly open. Two or three figures in black with bulletproof vests appeared and slowly crawled through the rows of seats to get closer to the stage without being seen. They were silent and had not slammed a door. I did not want to kiss the stage floor just yet. I coughed, trying to cover any noise that they were making. I hoped they would move a little faster!

Bob looked up with concern. "I hope you are not getting a cold up there. Of course," he smiled, "it would be your last!"

He is really crazy. How come none of us had noticed anything all these years?

"Anyway, back to Booth, since you are so curious. She was reading a book of our funds and expenses when I entered. I wore black and black sneakers. I have to admit, Maria, these cloaks that you got for the play are great for hiding under. They were really helpful in my travels throughout the school. Where was I?" he stopped. He started to turn to look at the seats. The police hit the floor silently.

I coughed again and spoke. God help me if he found the cops in here. I would be dead. "I was asking how you were able to make her murder look so nice and neat."

Bob looked up at me, turning his back on the police inching forward. Thank goodness! He laughed. "God Maria, I will miss your sense of humor as I am sitting on an island somewhere counting my drug funds! She had called me into her office the day before to yell at me about the loss of drug money for the month, and as she went on and on, I suddenly realized how pleasant the school would be without her. Booth was really nasty. I had been stealing funds from her for years and that month she had finally noticed! So, when her back was turned, and she looked at the ledger again to find something else to yell at me about, I took the letter opener from her desk. I then came back early the next morning, knowing she was meeting you. As she read the ledger I took out the letter opener from my pocket and stood behind her, and stabbed her, and stabbed her. I took the ledger. It was full of her blood. I burned it later in my backyard. Who knew that there were other copies? After she was dead, the school was very, very, quiet. I sat there with her dead body for a few minutes and enjoyed the quiet. It was a pleasure. I knew when you got there you would call the police, so I threw a cloak

into a plastic bag, took it with me and left the building. Do you want to know about Roberto?"
"Of course."
Can't those police crawl faster than this?
"I knew when Roberto would be going on stage in the blackout, because you and I had discussed the lighting the week before. So, I took the cloak and stepped up to him in the blackout and stabbed him. And thus, the world is short one very bad Hamlet performance, as we both know. Frankly, I was sorry about Roberto for a few days. I mean he was a student but business is business. Just like with the bomb I placed in your car. I was trying to get you to stop being so nosy." He shrugged. "I was a little angry about your students finding the cash in the dressing rooms. Booth had hidden it there and I couldn't find it. That money is lost to me. I'll just have to plan a shorter vacation. Oh well."
"Now onto what happened to Tommie the Newbie. When he discussed the funds at the prom, I realized that they had not sent a stupid principal to replace Booth. It was a shame, at least he was able to figure out the finances. I needed him out of the picture, because I was still draining money from her accounts. So, I knocked him out and stupid Sheila picked up the weapon. Boy, is that girl dim. That was great for me. I was outside having a smoke with the students while everyone was going crazy inside the prom. Sheila was perfect. I must send her some flowers when I get to where I am going. She really helped me

out! Then you became principal, I knew you were not a budget kind of gal, so I could fold up the business, take all the money I could and run. You would give me time."

I suppose this remark should have upset me, but I did not think about it because I was convinced I was going to die if the cops were not faster. Not a budget girl indeed! How did we not notice this guy was so very nuts in 20 odd years of teaching with us?

Also, I was not sure that you could send FTD to the mental health hospital for Sheila. I played my last question. The police looked really close to the edge of the stage now. "And Candy in the grave?"

"That is your last question I'm afraid. I am getting short of time and don't want to miss my plane. After this I must run. I need one last visit to Candy before I leave town. The last farewell, so to speak."

"Candy is a very needy greedy girl. She got on my nerves. Do you know she made a pass at me? She must be crazy! As if I did not know she was sleeping with everyone? As if I didn't worry about any diseases she could have? I got an idea to grab her after she left the school one evening by herself and decided after grabbing her that since Roberto's funeral was the next day, I could liven up the gravesite. She was easy to dump. Dump get it? Well, goodbye Maria. Sorry I can't stay to see you exit the stage." He laughed. It was not a pleasant sound.

He pressed the button.

I started to drop quickly. Bob ran for the backstage exit. Smith jumped on stage and tackled him. That girl was athletic! Viola ran for the button on the remote. He grabbed the control Bob had thrown down center stage. He stopped my downward drop from the fly. He gently lowered me to the stage floor. I started to cry. Bob was cursing as they hand-cuffed him and three cops had to hold onto him to lead him away. I could hear him cursing all the way to the police car.

The EMT people rushed in and carried out the injured security guard. He did not look good, but they informed me he was still breathing.

It took Viola half an hour to untie me. Bob had tied a lot of knots and used a lot of rope. I was still crying. Joe gave me tissues. When he got me free, he hugged me, hard. It was a very exciting moment, until I remembered Al at home worrying. I gently pushed Joe Viola away. "I need to call Al. He needs to know I am ok."

"I have police at your home. I called them while I was untying you. Al knows you are alright."

I was ok, except for some bruises and I still felt drugged. I sat down on the edge of the stage. I told Viola so. He yelled for EMT and they check me over for the third time in my life. They suggested I go home and sleep off the drug. I would have taken that idea if I did not know that Viola was going to the station to talk to Bob. I did not want to miss that conversation. I asked for

Viola's phone and spoke to Al telling him my plan to go back to the station with Viola. Al grunted at me. He was so angry he refused to talk. Viola nodded his head no. He did not want me to go with him to the station. But I walked out the side door carrying his phone. Viola came after me. I handed him back his phone. I climbed into his unmarked car. I had to see this through to the end. Nobody was happy.

36

The Interview

We got to Viola's office and he sent out for some good Italian coffee from the deli and some bakery goods from the Italian bakery close by. I ate three pastries filled with a million calories each. I was starving; not being killed did that to you. I would have to diet for a straight month to get off all of those calories.

Viola sat me in front of the one-way mirror facing the interview room and went into the main room to wait for Bob. Bob came in dressed in jailhouse orange. It was not a good color choice for him. I thought he looked better in the basic black cloak from the school play. In orange, he looked small and unimportant. Two police stood in back of his chair. He looked up at the one-way glass and smiled. It was like he knew I was there.

I shuddered. Smith walked in and sat next to me. She threw a coat that smelled of Viola's cologne around my shoulders. I stopped shaking as badly as before she walked in. I needed to find out what type of cologne Viola used. Maybe Al would like it. What was I thinking?

Viola asked Bob if he wanted water. Bob nodded yes. One of the police in the background headed for the door to get it for him. As he opened the door, a woman lawyer came in. She introduced herself to Viola as Bob's lawyer and sat next to him.

Bob turned to his lawyer. "They are accusing me of murders."

The lawyer demanded time with her client. Viola rose and the one policeman with him went out the door. The video and audio were turned off in the room. I sat facing a blank mirror. Viola came in. "My coat looks good on you."

I blushed.

He threw himself in an empty chair by Smith. "Now we wait."

And wait we did; for about an hour. The lawyer came out of the room and signaled to the police in the hallway. Viola walked down the hallway toward her. "My client has been advised not to talk to you. But he insists on doing so against my better judgment."

They both entered the room to face Bob.

The minute they sat down Bob turned to the mirror. "Hi, Maria, how are you doing? Can't wait to see you again." He started to laugh. He laughed and laughed and laughed. There was no stopping him. I did not realize until then how crazy he really was and how much he seemed to really hate me. Viola got up and used the phone in the room. He ordered a doctor to come to the interview room in the jail. Bob just laughed. Then he started to scream, "I killed them! I killed them! I killed them all!" I started to shake again. He was quite crazy. Smith threw her arm around me to calm me down.

The police grabbed Bob by his arms and took him still screaming to his cell. Viola looked at the lawyer. She shook her head and walked out of the room. Viola looked at me. "Smith, please take Maria home."

37

The Real Principal

I went home and stayed there for a week. The superintendent sent in a replacement substitute principal. Viola called to check on me and said Bob was going to be committed to an asylum for the criminally insane. He was quite mad. The superintendent told me since school was closed till July for summer school, and except for registration of new students, to take all the time off I needed. The substitute principal could handle the work over the summer. He was proud of my catching the killer. My desk would be waiting for me when I came back. I was not sure the first few days I would be coming back. As I sat there on my balcony overlooking traffic and strange people walking, the doorbell rang.

Of course, the doorman had not rung to say I had company some security! I asked through the door who it was. Jeff and the Nut Squad screamed that they were here! I let them in before the neighbors thought I had a bunch of crazy people in the hallway. All 20 of them came in. It was quite a crowd. My apartment living room was packed. They threw themselves on the floor and sat very close to each other. Jeff saved me a chair.

"Here, Teach!" he grabbed my hand and pushed me into the armchair. "I'm the spokespeople and the others and me got this great idea. We like really dug the Hamlet and the characters. From like reading it in class ya know? The characters like the way you explained them to us grabbed us, ya know? So, we all like got this idea for putting the play to music u know? We have been like missing you and Roberto and the play, ya know?" Martha started to cry. "Hey stop it ok?" She nodded and grabbed a Kleenex box off my coffee table. I knew I would never see that box again. "Anyway, we want you to hear this disc." He walked over to my smart TV and popped a disc in before I could even tell him how to turn it on. I should know by now the kids are better at electronics then I am. I sat back.

There was no escape till they were done with whatever they wanted to show me. I just hoped the apartment wasn't too damaged by then. Two girls went into my kitchen cabinets got out cookies and juice and served everyone. Glad I had enough supplies and glasses. Glad they didn't open the liquor up! Then out of the speakers came the nicest music I had ever heard the Nut Squad play. I was hearing for the first time their rendition of <u>Hamlet the Musical</u>. The music and singing went on for at least two hours. The kids all sat silent in my living listening to themselves sing their way through the whole play. It was wonderful. It was great. They were brilliant. I could not believe it. After the last note sounded I told them how grand and wonderful they were.

They applauded each other. They were so pleased. My poor neighbors! Jeff got silence again. "So, like, since the school is free and we need a fund raiser for our next year's senior trip, since only three of us graduated this year, we thought we would sell lots of tickets in our neighborhood and be able to like produce <u>Hamlet The Musical</u> in three or four weeks to raise money. That is, Teach, if you will come back and direct us? The music teacher was a big help, but he can't like, direct. Like, me and the others, we, like need you."

What educator would not agree to such a plan? The next day we started rehearsing on the same stage where Roberto was killed. It was not easy, but we all got it done together. There were bumps and problems in the rehearsal process and singers got sick but showed for opening night anyway. Jeff turned out to be a brilliant stage manager and ticket seller. I didn't know what he said to the students that he met that summer, but the whole senior class came to opening night. I was sure I didn't want to know what he had said. Al and Viola and Smith came to the opening night. The audience gave <u>Hamlet the Musical</u> a standing ovation. The students were thrilled.

And a surprise visitor, a Mr. Godard, also came to the opening night. He was president of a Tomato River cruise line. He had read about the musical and was a friend of the superintendent. He gave each of the performers a free month's cruise down the Seine to Monte Carlo in August for a class trip if they would do a Moliere play to music in sections at night for the passengers in his cabaret bar on the boat. What a wonderful gift! He also included tickets for Al and me. The cruise would give me time to think about my future, would it be with Al or Viola? I didn't know.

We all said yes. Jeff and the group were excited about writing another play to music. The superintendent was thrilled with the show and the trip. It would bring great publicity to the school. He thanked all the students individually for their fine work.

I walked the halls of the school with Smith, Viola, and Al. There seemed to be a positive air in the hallways that night. My show made $10,000 profit, which meant that the next year's play would have a great budget to use. I felt, walking through the school, that it was finally my school. I felt like a real principal. With all of us together, walking, the evening shadows in the hallway, I felt like I had come home at last.

The End

Made in the USA
Middletown, DE
10 August 2019